COMFORT AND JOI

8/05

For KAY -
ONE GREAT PIN-UP
DESERVES ANOTHER.

COMFORT AND JOI

Joseph Dougherty

iUniverse, Inc.
New York Lincoln Shanghai

Comfort and Joi

iUniverse books may be ordered through booksellers or by contacting:

iUniverse
2021 Pine Lake Road, Suite 100
Lincoln, NE 68512
www.iuniverse.com
1-800-Authors(1-800-288-4677)

ISBN: 0-595-33590-X

Printed in the United States of America

For Beverly
And Story Salon, where much of this began.

"A prime use of theory is to propose thoughts otherwise unthought."

—Raymond Durgnat

Contents

FRIDAY

While most sources claim Joi Lansing was born Joyce Wassmandoff or Was-mansdorff in Salt Lake City, Utah on April 6 of either 1928, 1929, 1933 or 1936, I found the Utah Historical Society identifies her as Joy Brown, the daughter of Virginia Shupe Brown, with 1928 being the most likely year of her birth. The name Brown disappears from the records and it is Joyce Wasmansdorff who arrived in Los Angeles with her devout Mormon parents in 1940.

Depending on which birth year you accept, the relocation occurred when Joi (whose first name would be spelled Joy until the mid-fifties) was anywhere between six and twelve. It's possible Joi arrived in Los Angeles as a six-year-old, but it's much more interesting to think of her making the move when she was on the brink of adolescence.

A twelve-year-old Joi, still a girl, but probably showing signs of the woman she would become, stepping from the train at Union Station is a powerful image. I suppose the Wasmansdorfs could have driven from Salt Lake City or taken the bus, but in the absence of evidence I'll assume they came by rail. Joi would have looked like one of those idyllic children who beamed out at you from Union Pacific ads in the pages of National Geographic. Boys in tweed suits and bow ties, girls in traveling dresses complete with little black patent-leather bags just like mother's.

When you look at Joi's early modeling work, pictures taken when she was still in her teens, it's not hard to imagine what she looked like as a child. If you ignore the lingerie, the boudoir setting and the come-hither look, you can extrapolate backwards. The round face, the soft cheeks and open green eyes widened by the excitement of the trip. You can see her between her parents, her white gloved hands in theirs, walking through that cathedral of a waiting room, toward the bright sunlight of a Los Angeles before freeways, where *The Wizard of Oz* was in the can, Orson Welles was preparing *Citizen Kane*, and the war in Europe was a concern only to intellectuals, communists and the ever growing number of emigrating Jews who were usually suspected members of the two previous groups.

Joi's physical development after moving to California was rapid and striking. She grew to five-foot, five-inches eventually filling out to her official measurements of 39-23-35. Still in high school at the close of The Second World War, sixteen-year-old Joi began work as a professional model.

There are two versions of how Joi broke into the movies, both involving film producer Arthur Freed. In one, Freed saw Joi in a high school play and signed her as a contract player at Metro-Goldwyn-Mayer. In the other version she entered a competition sponsored by M.G.M. to find new talent for the Fred Astaire-Judy Garland musical *Easter Parade*. In this second, slightly more credible telling, Joi was one of two hundred and fifty winners. She appeared as a model during the *Happy Easter* and *The Girl on the Magazine Cover* numbers.

The twenty-year-old was put under contract to M.G.M. in 1948 where her name became Joy Lansing. Enrolled in the studio's talent school she worked to develop her "poise and performing skills." She also came to the attention of the M.G.M. publicity department which would be the first of many such organizations to realize the photogenic blonde had value to the promotion of a motion picture independent of the amount of her screen time in the film. Throughout her career Joi would be more visible in the eight-by-tens, one-sheets and lobby cards advertising a movie than in the picture itself.

Typical of the M.G.M. hype was the publicity for *Take Me Out to the Ballgame* a 1949 musical from the Freed unit starring Gene Kelly (1912–1996) and Frank Sinatra (1915–1998). An M.G.M. press release touted that a group of 2,500 young men from Boston had supposedly named Joi "The Girl We Would Most Like to Take to the Ballgame."

Her work in this picture, as with the bulk of her M.G.M. projects, was uncredited. While her role was described by one source as "microscopic" it does represent her first crossing with Frank Sinatra who would weave through the later years of her life. We don't know if they actually met on this picture.

The M.G.M. publicity department probably engineered Joi's appearance on the cover of Life Magazine on March 28, 1949. It's difficult to describe to anyone under forty the importance Life Magazine once had. In an era before television an appearance in Life, especially on its cover, meant your ascendancy. Whatever the field, you had arrived because the weekly found you worthy of note. If you know Joi only from her mature bombshell period, you might not recognize her here. She looks up and out from the black-and-white cover photo, her blonde hair swept back, not yet platinum. Her face still has the rounded softness of a teenager.

Joi is described in the cover story as the girl silent film producer Hal Roach (1892–1992) selected after a restaurant encounter to play the "dumb blonde" in a series of short films he hoped to produce for the questionable medium of television. According to the article Joi, "a latter day combination of Thelma Todd and Jean Harlow," was to appear in the *Sadie and Sally* series of twenty-six minute films made on two-day schedules for the miniscule budget, even by 1949 standards, of $8,500 a piece. Roach hoped, "Her well-rounded good looks and engagingly sexy flair for slapstick comedy roles will make her one of television's leading light-headed characters."

Condescending tone aside, Roach was accurate in his prediction, although the lost *Sadie and Sally* shorts wouldn't be the vehicle of that success.

Having finally played a character with a name (Linda. Uncredited. *Neptune's Daughter*, 1949) Joi was dropped from the M.G.M. roster when her contract came up for renewal in 1950. This ended not only a succession of incrementally larger roles, but cut her off from the juggernaut of M.G.M. publicity. Joi had to learn the art of self-promotion.

In 1950, she entered and won the Miss Hollywood Beauty Contest and toured U.S. Armed Forces bases in Japan, Europe and North Africa. As a freelance actress she moved between major studio productions and low-budget pictures in what became a life-long pattern. There was also a return to modeling assignments.

In 1951, Joi married actor Lance Fuller (1928–2001). The marriage was brief and tumultuous ending in divorce in 1953. Information about the marriage is sketchy with references to "unpleasant newspaper coverage" and the gossipy suggestion of acrimony and public confrontations.

Lance Fuller had a feature career analogous to Joi's, rarely rising above bit parts and walk-ons and then only in minor low-budget features. His acting style can charitably be described as minimal. Fuller's memories of his marriage to Joi Lansing are self-serving and often inaccurate. In interviews Fuller seems uncertain when he was married to the actress, claiming they were together "during the forties," or for how long, "It was about ten years, but we had a separation so it was more like three years." He also places her in the titular number of the Gene Kelly-Stanley Donan production *Singin' in the Rain*. Joi was in the film, but not in the famous number.

It's likely professional jealousy on the part of Fuller was at least one source of conflict in the marriage. Joi Lansing and Lance Fuller were arguably at the same level in the entertainment hierarchy, but Joi would have had a natural career advantage in being both female and beautiful. While Fuller was not unattractive, his features reflecting English, French and Cherokee heritage, extraneous men weren't added to movies because of their looks. Women were and still are. Fuller standing at the bar in some night club set with a drink in his hand would simply be part of the human background you never notice in a movie. Joi at the bar would have been something more.

The Assistant Director sees a gap in the Background Artists at the bar, a hole that could subliminally snag the audience and distract it from the foreground action. He can put in a relatively handsome man in a blue suit, or he can set Joi in the place. The choice is simple. No one in the history of American movies was ever fired for putting another pretty girl in the picture.

So Joi is placed at the bar, told to interact silently with the extras on either side of her. Costumed lavishly or provocatively depending on the scene, she would shimmer as Background and then Action are called. Laughing without a sound, drinking her prop drink, smoking her prop cigarette, not inhaling since her Mormon faith forbids tobacco, she'd sense the bulk of the Technicolor camera brushing by her, dollying through the room on its way to discover the hero's cautious entrance or the heroine's return from the powder room after a good cry.

The shot is repeated several times, then the scene is repeated from different angles. Joi makes the same moves with the cigarette, takes the same sips from the fake cocktail, laughs gaily to the same unheard joke, so everything will match when cut together.

Between takes she relaxes, but stays in position. She looks through the bottles against the mirror behind the bar. Over the shoulder of her reflection she sees the black void of the soundstage beyond the edges of the set. Salt Lake City would have seemed so far away at moments like this. She might have thought about how far she'd come, how much she'd accomplished. But was this as far as she could expect to go? Five lines or under on a good day?

After five hours the three page scene is completed. Joi thanks the Assistant Director for choosing her and not someone else. The acknowledgment might be a word or a touch or a smile. In any case she will be remembered and brought back, having made the sort of impression her husband was incapable of making.

It's odd going back to look at movies I've seen a hundred times after learning Joi was in there someplace as an extra. Your perception changes as your eyes focus on the crowds instead of the principals. And suddenly there she is, blonde and curvaceous and often smiling, part of the Bruegel landscape that fills the frame.

Why didn't I see her before? What else have I missed out of the corner of my eye?

Once free of Lance Fuller it would be six years before Joi remarried. After the divorce she lived alone in a house in Burbank and continued to work on her acting skills at the University of California in Los Angeles. She won small roles during the early fifties playing Cigarette Girl, Model, Bathing Girl in Dream, Showgirl, and Blonde in Boarding House. Lansing's name appears on a preliminary list of actresses being considered to play Miss Caswell, Addison DeWitt's companion in *All About Eve* (20th Century-Fox, 1950), a part that would go to Marilyn Monroe. Joi lost at least one other role to Monroe, that of Angela Phinlay, the mistress of Louis Calhern's character in *The Asphalt Jungle* (M.G.M., 1950).

Single and without a studio contract, small roles supplemented by modeling assignments, the period of the early fifties must have been one of great disappointment. Still in her early twenties, Joi's career in features had stalled well below expectations. As Hal Roach predicted, it was television that rescued her.

In 1955, Lansing came to the attention of Al Simon, producer of *The George Burns and Gracie Allen Show*. Simon was sufficiently impressed by Joi's talents and appearance to create a role for her on his new project, a half-hour comedy about "a girl chasing Hollywood fashion photographer" played by another refugee from shrinking feature opportunities, Robert Cummings (1908–1990). *The Bob Cummings Show*, or *Love That Bob* as it was called in endless syndication reruns, would eventually total one hundred and seventy-five episodes produced between 1955 and 1959. Joi appeared in one hundred and twenty-five shows as Shirley Swanson, Bob's favorite model. A character with both a first and last name.

Although she would later dismiss her role as "a job wearing sweaters," the popular series became the backbone of a television career extending well into the 1960s. Joi made guest appearances on numerous series including *Sea Hunt*, *Maverick*, *Perry Mason*, and *The Untouchables*. At one point she was in competition with herself, appearing in two different anthology dramas on two different networks broadcast at the same time (November 17, 1955; *Four Star Theater* on CBS, *Ford Theater* on NBC). By 1956 she had become such a familiar television presence that she appeared on an episode of *I Love Lucy* playing the part of "Joi Lansing."

The impact of all this television work on her feature career was negligible. There were some interesting spikes including *The Brave One* (RKO, 1956), a film remembered primarily for the embarrassment it caused the Academy of Motion Picture Arts and Sciences when it won the Oscar for Best Original Story by blacklisted writer Dalton Trumbo writing under the pseudonym Robert Rich. And while she is an integral part of Orson Welles' *Touch of Evil* (Universal-International, 1958) she is essentially unrecognizable. These curiosities aside, Joi's feature work consists largely of bottom-of-the-bill second features to which she brought a radiance unmerited by their budgets.

On August 5, 1960, Joi married thirty-seven-year old investment broker Stanley Todd who had been serving as her business manager for several years.

This brings up the question of Jerry Safron. Safron appears at the bottom of the list of spouses in Joi's entry on the Internet Movie Database. There are no dates for the alleged marriage which is indicated as ending in divorce.

An unambiguous statement that Joi was married only once before Todd can be found in the National Enquirer of September 25, 1960. The cover of the issue is given over to a full-length image of Joi, a retouched promotional still for *Hot Cars* (United Artists, 1956), and the headline: "Joi Lansing Tried To Win Her Man's Heart Through His Stomach But Says–I Nearly Cooked My Romance Instead of the Dinner."

The article states, "It's Stan's first marriage and her second." Joi elaborates, "In a way, that's an advantage. He's the kind who if he had one bad experience would run like Seabiscuit from even the thought of another hitch in servitude. Women are different. About marriage, anyway. Since it's the only state in which we're honestly happy, we're optimistic about wedded bliss."

While this Runyonesque quote sounds like the work of a press agent, I'm inclined to believe the two marriage count. In spite of the fact that elsewhere in the issue there's a photograph of a man who tried to shoot off his own head with a shotgun and Criswell's prediction that Zsa Zsa Gabor would be elected mayor of a west coast city in 1966, I find the National Enquirer more credible than something I got off the internet.

With the marriage to Todd came an attempt to forge a new career. Joi's voice was a rich and mellow one, unlike the brassy sandpaper or breathy whisper of other "dumb" blondes. She also knew how to carry a tune and sell a song. An emphasis on singing coincided with the brief appearance of the Scopitone machine, a coin operated video juke box that ran short 16 mm sound movies, the precursor of the music video. Joi's attributes made her a natural for the format. Dubbed "The Scopitone Bombshell," she appeared in several of the company's mini-production numbers, often touring to promote the devices. Scopitone went out of business in November 1969. The machines that didn't end up in junkyards were reconditioned to show industrial training films and peepshow loops.

Joi Lansing is thought to have undergone breast augmentation surgery in the early 1960s, increasing her bust to forty-one inches. A comparison of pictures taken in the late fifties and poses from the mid-sixties reveal something dramatic has indeed happened.

Developed in 1943, liquid polymer silicone was first used for breast enlargement in wartime Japan when cosmetologists injected the substance directly into the breasts of prostitutes. The first silicone gel implants, consisting of liquid silicone contained in a thicker silicone shell or capsule, were used by Texas plastic surgeons Dr. Thomas D. Cronin and Dr. Frank J. Gerow in 1963. The standardized procedure for inserting the implants was through a side incision either in front of the gland or behind the muscle.

Joi's television work continued, including a recurring role on *The Beverly Hillbillies* as Gladys Flatt, the fictional wife of title song co-balladeer Lester Flatt, but she would appear in no theatrical films between 1960 and 1965.

The end of her feature career is closely associated with Frank Sinatra and Dean Martin.

Sinatra hired Joi to appear in his ABC variety show broadcast in February, 1958 from the El Capitan Theater on Hollywood Boulevard. There was a relationship between the singer and the actress the exact nature of which is not known, but it did lead to her being cast in *A Hole in the Head* with Sinatra in 1959. The following year she worked with brother Rat Packer Dean Martin in *Who Was That Lady?* (Columbia Pictures, 1960) and later with both Martin and Sinatra in *Marriage on the Rocks* (Warner Bros.,1965), Joi Lansing's last appearance in a major studio movie.

By the mid-sixties the blonde bombshell was experiencing a steady decline from archetype to cliché, fast approaching hibernation in the chilly face of early feminism's cultural revolution. Marilyn Monroe died of a drug overdose in 1962 at the age of thirty-six. Later, critics would metaphorically break into Monroe's crypt in Westwood, steal the relics and set her up as some sort of slutty saint, symbolic of whatever a particular theorist was thinking at the moment. Jayne Mansfield was killed in a car wreck driving between low rent personal appearances five years later. The purpose of Mansfield's parody died with Monroe and Jayne would be denied deification. Largely forgotten today, she became the mangled punchline to somebody else's joke. Robbed of such mythic ends, lesser examples such as Mamie Van Doren and Diana Dors slipped into middle-age and obscurity.

But those blondes had their bosoms on the front line, top-billed in their movies. One of the reasons Joi managed to survive was that she was rarely at the center of the movies she was in. She was not a loadbaring element in the studio produced movies and therefore not responsible for the success or failure of the piece. She couldn't ruin a movie, she could only improve it by smiling and leaning over.

Prettier than Mansfield, more stable than Monroe, Joi Lansing soldiered on in the trenches, an affordable third choice for a role, often becoming the only memorable thing in the movies that surrounded her, where the size of her billing was inversely proportionate to the budget.

In 1965, her feature career effectively over, Joi debuted her nightclub act at New York City's Living Room Club. The evening of light comedy and popular songs, including a Sinatra medley, was well received. One critic reviewing her at Manhattan's Copacabana described her singing voice and stage presence as a "revelation." Another review described her entrance: "Joi saunters up to the mike in the most daring gown in all of show business. The bottom half of her dress clings to her slender gams like wet tissue paper, and the top half—well, there almost is no top half. It roughly approximates two wide shoulder straps joined somewhere in the neighborhood of her navel, and it is filled to over-flowing with a figure that makes Jayne Mansfield look like Fred Astaire."

According to The New York Journal-American, Lansing "has taken a giant step toward singing stardom." This "giant step" resulted in bookings at the Cork Club in Houston, Texas and the Diplomat in Hollywood, Florida.

At the age of forty, Joi concentrated on nightclubs and dinner theaters. She performed an eight week run of *Gentlemen Prefer Blondes* at The Memphis

Civic Theater in 1968. In the summer of 1969 she appeared in the revue *Follies Burlesque '69* in Latham, New York and in 1970 performed in a production of Neil Simon's *Come Blow Your Horn* at The Thunderbird Hotel in Las Vegas.

She told an interviewer that year she was hoping for "time to sit things out and see which way the wind will blow, what the new trends will be. Frankly, I'm confused."

Joi Lansing was diagnosed with breast cancer in 1970 and underwent surgery early that summer.

Some believe she went back to work after a brief recuperation, shooting the extremely low-budget horror movie *Big Foot* for director Robert Slatzer, who later claimed to have been married to Marilyn Monroe. I have doubts about the sequence of these events.

Late in 1970 Joi was hired for a dinner theater production of the British sex farce *Pajama Tops*, but illness forced her to leave the production during rehearsals. Joi signed to star in a new production of *Follies Burlesque* at the Meadowbrook Theater in New Jersey scheduled to open in late July of 1972. As preparations for the production were under way she discovered her cancer had returned, complicated by severe anemia.

On July 1, Joi Lansing was admitted to St. John's Hospital in Santa Monica, California. She died there on the evening of Monday, August 7, 1972 at the age of forty-four, two days after her twelfth wedding anniversary.

She is buried in Santa Paula Cemetery in Ventura County, north of Los Angeles.

Joi once told a reporter: "I am not how I look inside. Outside, I'm blonde and fluffy, but inside I do have a heart and soul and deep feelings. Yet no one gives me credit personally, because of the exterior. My being blonde and curvy you might say, was a kind of mixed blessing. I was always known as a glamour girl and categorized only as that. It was very limiting. I was held back by my image."

Joi Lansing is a cultural artifact from a time of bolder symbolism, when you knew the level of a character's sexual experience by the saxophones on the soundtrack when she walked into a room. Her progression from cheesecake model to extra to starlet was not an unusual one. It was a path followed with varying degrees of success by hundreds if not thousands of girls who managed to get to Hollywood in the late forties and early fifties. Why write about this one and not some other? I don't have an answer other than this is the one who stuck in my mind. But that's not exactly true.

Yes, I saw the movies she was in, but I wasn't really aware of her at the time. At least not consciously. I can't reach back and find the exact moment I first became aware of Joi Lansing. I must have seen her when I was a child watching *The Adventures of Superman*. I remember the episode in which Joi played an undercover police woman named Sgt. Helen O'Hara who poses as the Man of Steel's wife. The episode opens on a small civil ceremony with Lois Lane watching from a corner and looking miserable about the proceedings. It's a phony marriage, of course, designed to catch some gangsters.

There's another image I remember from the episode. A two-shot of Joi facing George Reeves (1914–1959) in his Superman outfit. There's Joi, resplendently blonde, her lipstick as red as the big "S" on George's chest. They seemed like a very balanced couple to me, both icons, both much more powerful than mere mortals, both here to make the world a better place.

No wonder Lois Lane was jealous. Projecting a sexuality as burnished as her platinum hair, Joi's presence in a scene drained femininity from the women around her. Her eyes always seemed smart and direct. Even in the silliest of cheesecake poses, and I've seen some doozies, there's a playful reality to her expression and posture; a self awareness of her lovely face and spectacular figure that communicated to me the sense that she was having as much fun looking like that as you were having looking at her.

But that's all subjective, isn't it? Phrases like "burnished sexuality" don't have any real meaning. Instead of explaining how I feel they crash to the floor like sash weights.

Standing on the deck outside the dining room of Mark and David's house I wonder if there are other men in other borrowed vacation homes between me and the beach, working out their low-grade obsessions with Allison Hayes, Mala Powers, Yvette Vickers or Peggy Castle. This seems unlikely. It's November and most of the houses around me in this part of Oxnard are empty; garages shut, unswept sand in the driveways.

I think there's life in the house next door on the ocean side. Early this morning I woke up in Mark and David's continent of a bed surrounded by colorless predawn light. I heard the opening and closing of a car door, then the unlocking of the house and sounds of someone making two trips back and forth for luggage. Then a beep to turn on a car alarm and the closing of the front door.

I tried to go back to sleep, but ended up leaning against the pillows, watching the room emerge from the gloom.

I could just make out my computer bag and knapsack filled with DVDs and cassettes on the chair with my jacket where I dropped them last night, my duffel on the floor in front of them. My things looked foreign and rumpled in this room. I probably looked rumbled in that bed.

There is nothing like spending time with homosexual men to make you feel frumpy, woebegone and incapable of making anything but the worst possible choice in matters of attire and haircut. I suppose if there is a gay agenda it must be to make heterosexual men look like some hastily executed rough draft for the male of the species. A galumphing prototype that went on to physical and emotional perfection in a model so polished and self-defining that only members of its own kind can satisfy it. Sometimes I catch women looking at these perfect men and sighing at the masculine glory denied them because they lacked the foresight to be born with penises of their own.

Mark and David tolerate me at the edge of their circle. I often feel like a pet, or a foster child from some backward country without personal trainers or rejuvenating skin care products.

"She's very minor, isn't she?"

"Is there actually enough there for a book?"

"Maybe you should open it up more. You could talk to Donald."

Donald being a friend of theirs who owns a room full of Marilyn Monroe memorabilia including several gowns and the check she signed on the day she overdosed. "Her last autograph," he whispers as he shows you the yellowing document in its frame.

"What exactly are you trying to prove by writing about her?"

This last more a challenge than a question. The implication being I need to be vetted before I can write about this woman from my past. As if gays held exclusive salvage rights to popular culture and I was threatening to poach on their turf.

"I don't think I'm trying to *prove* anything. I wasn't even aware I was all that interested in her till I turned around one day and noticed the tapes on the shelf, next to all the stills and magazines. Obsessions sneak up on you, like snowdrifts."

"Well, I suppose you'll just have to work through it somehow."

"He could go up to the beach house and work on it. We won't be using it till after Christmas."

"What a scathingly brilliant idea. You could go up there, be by yourself and see what you've got. If anything."

"Take a weekend. That should be plenty of time to find out one way or the other. You're not doing anything right now, are you?"

"No."

"Go up there with your tapes and pictures and rough the project out. You might be able to write the whole thing; there aren't many distractions in Oxnard in November."

The offer seemed generous, but was I tricked into Mark and David's over-sized movie star bed and set up to fail?

"Poor baby. Look who he picks to idolize: A tea-totaling Mormon. A bit player who wasn't able to fuck her way to the middle."

"He'll learn what becomes a legend most when he tries to stretch *that* into a book."

No, Joi Lansing will never achieve legendary status. Whatever her life was it wasn't a strident opera of scandal and substance abuse. She lacked the self-destructive impulses required for tabloid immortality. Even her contact with Sinatra and Martin seems to be without much innuendo, depending on how you feel about Kitty Kelley. It strikes me that I've hitched my wagon to The Rat Pack's designated driver.

But she was one of the working stiff character actors who made American movies and early television a sort of extended family for me. That may not be much, but it should count for something.

So, I'm going to spend the next few days alone with Joi Lansing here in Oxnard. I'll look at her movies on disk and cassette, at her photographs, at the magazines and books and internet material I've stumbled on or looked for, all the things that started out as clutter, but seem to have become a collection. I'm going to treat the disposable as if it were the important, swap the foreground for the background and see what happens.

If I don't do this for her, who will?

Joi Lansing's face wasn't a collection of wedges and plains, but something softer. When you look at those early pin-ups you notice her full cheeks, often accentuated by a wide smile. Their roundness would always be with her, but it's particularly striking in the early pictures, reminding you just how young she was.

Kewpie doll cheeks. There's at least one photo of her posing with two such dolls close to her face to reinforce the connection. Like the cheeks on The Campbell Soup Kids. Are the Campbell Soup Kids still working or have they been retired, sent to the showers with the Sinclair dinosaur and Speedy Alka-Seltzer?

The Campbell Soup Kids were a pair of cherubic children drawn for magazine ads and later animated for television commercials who symbolized the wholesome goodness of Campbell products. "M'mm, m'mm good." A boy and a girl with no parents in evidence, their primary facial feature was their rosy cheeks, so shinny and round and taut, they appeared to be under great pressure.

I hope the Campbell Company phased them out. If they'd been kept around they would have been forced to undergo a grotesque updating to make them more contemporary. The sort of process that changed Aunt Jemima from an unauthorized caricature of Hattie McDaniels into a deeply tanned Donna Reed.

Never mind the Campbell Soup Kids, who remembers Donna Reed or Hattie McDaniels?

This is a problem I'm having more and more as I lurch into my fifties. All my references, all my cultural shorthand is becoming obsolete, like a language spoken by a rapidly diminishing tribe of Pacific islanders. I don't think I'd mind, or maybe I'd mind less, if they were being replaced with something of equal eloquence, but that's not happening. Lately, everything seems drained of meaning.

Maybe it's the rapid turnover now, or how pride has leached out of everything. America no longer has the patience or expertise to make its own shoes, no wonder the culture is so lame. Compared to the glue-gun constructions of life today, there's an old world craftsmanship in the making of what was disposable when I was growing up.

I realize there's no convincing way to talk about this without sounding like a wizened nostalgic clinging to the past because that's where he last saw his youth. But I think what drives that argument is that the people in charge today are aware of how thin the cultural soup has become, and if they acknowledge it, even for a second, all would be chaos. So they artificially inflate the value of the present culture in order to protect their investment. One of the ways they do this is by dismissing everything that came before as worthless, slow and reeking of the grave.

The benefits here are manifold. For one, it saves you from ever having to learn anything; since there's nothing relevant back there, there's nothing worth studying. A bonus is that you can look like a genius when you invent something brand new that's been around for forty or fifty years.

When Joi relaxes the smile, the cheeks are diminished and she looks at the camera with something more challenging. Regardless of expression there's an awareness of you looking at her.

Joi by the pool; Joi in a bathing suit framed in a Spanish arch; Joi in a black nightgown hugging her pillow; Joi in a white nightgown set against a wall of padded leather; Joi, legs folded under her, sitting on a satin bed with a huge headboard cut in the shape of an artist's palette, her peignoir off the near shoulder and kept from falling farther by the slope of her breasts; Joi in shorts and a tight sweater turned to accent a bullet-shaped silhouette, looking at us as if amused to be discovered in such a conical condition. Joi, her chest alternatively lifted and projected by miracles of engineering, or unfettered and barely concealed by folds of confectionary fabric. She favors no side, her face equally pretty from the right, the left or straight on.

Hundreds of shots selected from ten times as many rolls of film. The result of days and months in photographers' studios.

"You feel, the first few times, like a lamb led to the slaughter. But the photographer takes care of that," she remembered in an interview. "He moves around you, studying you, and then he tells you how to sit or stand. 'More leg there,' he'll say. Or, 'Lower the bra a trifle. Smile! Give 'em that old allure.'"

Which she did, patiently and professionally, either posed in a sweater holding a hammer and broken mirror under a ladder with Friday the Thirteenth on
a calendar, or leaning over an antique typewriter in one of the countless shots
taken of her in a polka-dot bikini for *Marriage on the Rocks*. She is never less
than appealing, usually much more.

How are these picture intrinsically different from the tens of thousands of
other cheesecake shots of other models? If I say there's something genuine in
her face, if I say she seems present in the instant of the open shutter, then I'm
back to being subjective. Do I like her shots better because of this honesty I
detect, or do I detect the honesty because I like the shots better?

I have to remind myself these photos weren't meant to be overly analyzed,
or analyzed at all, really. They were disposable products of commerce. Any
artistic status they have now was acquired retroactively and defensively.

I'm not interested in making the case for girly pictures. That's an unwinna-
ble debate that can end in shrieky accusations of socially sanctioned rape. I
know people who've been publicly denounced for allowing a Victoria's Secret
catalogue into their home, so I don't want to engage anyone over Joi in a barrel
attired in nothing but soap bubbles. I do worry about people who think a lingerie catalogue is pornography. I'm concerned about what will happen to their
brains if they ever encounter the real thing.

Knowing that I risk the wrath of the sexual Khmer Rouge, I continue to find
pictures of Joi Lansing in her idealized sleepwear and tight sweaters pleasing to
the eye and soothing to the spirit. There's a sweetness to them, a sort of
informed innocence. I believe the authority to enjoy these images comes from
the lady herself. I believe you can see it in her eyes.

Mark and David's house isn't actually on the beach, it's on a street of vacation homes built perpendicular to the shore. You reach the water by walking a block then crossing a street and going through an undeveloped lot between two massive and unattractive houses. As a rule, the closer you get to the water, the bigger and uglier the houses. Ahead is a green stretch of the Pacific and, out on the horizon, the Channel Islands. The surf is weak, the November sky gray. A mile north along the coast there's a massive collection of towers and smoke stacks. The Mandalay Generating Facility, according to the gate I passed driving to the house last night. To the south are more brutish homes and clusters of condominiums.

There's a marina beyond the power plant with a couple of not terrible restaurants mixed with shops selling kites, frozen yogurt and overpriced art reproductions. I know how to find the gas station and the Vons and expect to survive the weekend without much effort. If I get bored there's Ventura and, farther up the 101, Santa Barbara, beyond the juncture with the 126 which will take me to Santa Paula and Joi Lansing's grave.

Walking back to the house from the beach I saw the car I heard arrive early this morning. It wasn't there when I left for my walk. It's a dark blue Volvo station wagon, not new, with California plates, parked on the pale concrete driveway that blends into the drive in front of Mark and David's house where my Civic is parked.

The house next door looks like a rough mirror of the one I'm staying in: Double garage doors, a gate to a walkway leading to the entrance of the two-story house, a deck built over the garage. It's yellow color is vibrant in the cloudy light. Mark and David's is salmon with deeper pink trim.

If the inside of that house is anything like the inside of mine, the first floor will be two small bedrooms, a guest bath, a laundry room with a side door, and a door to the garage. A staircase leads from the entrance up to a large living room spilling into a dining room opening on one side to the deck with the opposite end blending into a kitchen with a preparation island in the middle. A hall leads to the back of the house, to Mark and David's bedroom and bathroom.

The furniture is covered with sheets to keep the dust off. This surprised me last night. I always thought that was a movie convention meant to suggest abandonment and absence. The only time I've ever seen it in reality was when I was a small child.

My grandmother was a housekeeper for one of the fading families on the North Shore of Long Island. My grandfather served in the Dickensian role of groom in their stables. I remember my mother leaving me in my grandmother's care one day and my going with her to this great closed house surrounded by woods. My grandmother made a tuna salad sandwich for me in the kitchen then sent me off to wander.

The family was off somewhere and the rooms were cold. Sheets covered elephantine sofas and spindly Windsor chairs. Winter light came through French windows and reflected painfully off the dark walnut floors. When that house shows up in my dreams the floors are what I remember, probably because I was closer to them at the time, and the way the light hurt my eyes.

I'm not sure how many times I was there. At first I thought it was quite often, now I wonder if it was only once. There was only the one tuna sandwich. My grandmother meant well, but it came out oily, dark and lumpy and not at all the way my mother prepared tuna.

What's the purpose of remembering something like that? Why should one disappointing tuna sandwich rate immortality?

Since Mark and David's thirty-six inch television and video players are in the bedroom I expect that's where I'll be spending most of my time and can keep my sheet disturbing to a minimum.

Joi did uncredited work in several Metro-Goldwyn-Mayer pictures, but *Singin' in the Rain*, made in 1952, is the best overall movie and the most widely seen. Most of the movies Joi worked in are sufficiently obscure to require plot synopsis. *Singin' in the Rain* is the exception.

Although missing from the on-screen credits, Joi is listed in the cast in the 1972 published edition of the Betty Comden and Adolph Green script. Near the bottom, between Valle Impersonator and Fencers comes Audience: Dorothy Patrick, William Lester, Charles Evans, Joi Lansing. Joi with an "i" which wouldn't have been how she spelled it at the time of the film's release.

She appears on-screen for less than a minute in total, has no dialogue and if you weren't looking for her with the remote in your hand you wouldn't see her. She's an extra. Yet this extra gets her name in a book published the year she died. I saw the movie for the first time around then as part of a double-bill at a revival house.

The wonderful thing about revival house double-bills was that you went for the movie you liked, stayed for something you never heard of, and usually came out loving the second feature more than the one you'd gone to see. That was the generous conspiracy a good revival house worked on its regulars and that's how I saw *Singin' in the Rain*. I don't remember the movie I went to see.

It was a dangerous time to like Hollywood musicals, especially one as unrepentantly life affirming as *Singin' in the Rain*. This was the year after Stanley Kubrick staged Malcolm McDowell's a cappella version of the title song as accompaniment for a beating and rape in *A Clockwork Orange*. The song, and by association the movie, picked up an almost lethal subtext loaded with postmodern cynicism that threatened to overwhelm the original and make it impossible to enjoy.

I remember thinking it was a pretty cheap shot on Kubrick's part, an easy joke at the expense of a better movie. Once the Kubrick film lost its topicality things slowly evened out and reputations have stabilized. But you were asking for trouble in the era of *Easy Rider* to claim affection for a vintage studio produced musical. They could be evoked as sarcastic reference points, examples of an earlier generation's neurotic drive to escape reality, but you couldn't *like* them.

And *Singin' in the Rain* insists that you like it. Frame for frame you won't find a more honest movie; one that never drops back to an ironic safe distance. This is one of the reasons it still works. And it does work, especially if you can see it with an audience which is next to impossible now.

Joi first appears early in the picture when Gene Kelly arrives at the home of the studio head after the premiere of *The Royal Rascal*. Kelly enters the house and is surrounded by well-wishers. Joi is one of the people rushing up to him. She enters from the left side of the frame wearing a pale dress, her blonde hair in flapper style (the film is set in 1927) under a rhinestone crusted headband, two tiny platinum spit curls at each temple. Donald O'Connor (1925–2003) arrives, taking Kelly deeper into the party. The camera goes with them, panning off Joi and the others.

You can see her again more clearly a few minutes later, just after the studio head shows the demonstration of "a talking picture." The lights come up and Joi is in the background on a settee. In the foreground, studio head R.F. Simpson (Millard Mitchell), Director Roscoe Dexter (Douglas Fowley), and Rod, the publicity man (King Donovan) have an exchange about the future of sound films. Joi stands and crosses behind them, clearing the shot by the time Donald O'Connor folds in next to the other men to button the exchange.

She's in the shot about seven seconds, just filling in the background with a cross. But if you focus on her, if you do the opposite of what's expected and ignore the foreground, you get to watch her surprisingly serious face and what she's doing with her eyes. She tracks Rod, the publicity man, giving us a chance to spin all sorts of backstory for her. Did he invite her to the party? Is she expecting him to introduce her to the director and the studio head? If so, she's disappointed. Rod doesn't acknowledge her at all. Her eyes click over to the studio chief then she turns away and exits. All that bonus drama in a seven second background cross.

This suggests some interesting entertainment possibilities. What would happen if we watched movies by tracking the extras, as if theirs were the stories we'd paid to see? Each movie has the potential of becoming hundreds of movies. Choose carefully and one picture might last a lifetime as you follow all those fragmented dramas in other cars, at different tables, on the far side of hotel lobbies, crossing streets, crowding elevators.

The actor she's looking at is King Donovan (1918–1987) who would play Harvey Helm, a recurring character along with her on *The Bob Cummings Show* three years later. Did they talk after this scene? When they worked on the Cummings show did either one remember the earlier cross?

Near the end of *Singin' in the Rain*, Joi can be found in the audience at the premiere of *The Dancing Cavalier*. She has an aisle seat and is wearing the same wardrobe she wore at the party. When *The Dancing Cavalier* ends and the audience clamors for its stars to take a bow you can find Joi at the left of a wide shot as Lena Lamont (Jean Hagen, 1923–1977) comes on stage and speaks to the crowd in a voice which has become synonymous with dumb blonde actresses ever since.

As Lena talks, the movie cuts to Joi again. We've crossed the axis from the previous wide shot and discover her in a tighter shot of six people in two rows. She's on the left again, reacting to how Lena doesn't sound at all like she did in the movie she just saw.

The young man sitting next to Joi (her date?) yells to the actress on stage, "Cut the talk, Lena! Sing?"

The wide shot is used again when Kathy Selden (Debbie Reynolds, b. 1932) starts to sing for Lena from behind the theater curtain and a third time after Kelly and O'Connor open the curtain to reveal the real source of the singing voice. That third time, once the trick has been revealed, shows the audience in on the joke and laughing at Lena. Joi has committed to a huge, boisterous, explosion of a belly laugh. We can't hear her in the mix, but we can see how loud she's laughing. Before they cut out of the shot, Joi bends forward, doubling over with hysteria at the edge of the image.

She's been at the edge of that frame for more than half a century, laughing. There every time I've seen the movie and I never noticed. No reason to, really. Her contribution to the film is, indeed, microscopic. But when you focus the microscope on her it's amazing how deeply committed she is to that laugh. This is acting on the molecular level, jazzing around with the genetic material of the movie well below the supposed limits of perception.

Joi Lansing didn't have an acting career so much as a re-acting career. Even when she did have dialogue and a character with at least a first name, most of her screen time consists of listening, sometimes when addressed directly, but often to musical numbers, or arguments between more important characters. Not only is she pretty to look at, a relief from whatever else is trying to happen, she's a useful emotional signpost, indicating how we should take a certain event or piece of information.

"This terrible country western song is very pleasing."

"I comprehend your description of the other person in this scene as a wolf and confirm his sexual desirability."

"Yes, your friend is acting oddly. Perhaps he is deeply troubled by earlier scenes of conflict that would seem formulaic and unconvincing were it not for how seriously I'm reacting."

"You are handsome."

"That is dangerous."

"He is funny."

She's a sort of translator, a slinky gloss explaining a muddled text.

It's also another place of connection between Joi and the rest of us. We spend so much of our lives reacting, accommodating instead of instigating. Always returning volleys without ever winning service.

There's a convenience store in the strip mall walking distance from the house, but I decided to take the ten minute drive to the big Vons. Strip mall isn't the right term for the collection of cinderblock buildings; that would indicate a sense of planning. The convenience store (MILK-LIQUOR-LOTTO), coin laundromat and dark windowed video rental shop look like things left behind, forgotten by travelers who pulled over, tossed them out, then drove on as fast as possible.

The Vons, which you get to be making a left, a right at the gas station, then a three mile run through cultivated fields, past a small airport for small planes with what looks like an ornamental control tower stolen from a miniature golf course, sits on one corner of an intersection built for commerce. Around the compass are another gas station, one of those boisterous family restaurants where they summon you to your table with a vibrating pager, and a commercial mall with real estate offices, donut shop and a Salvation Army Thrift Store.

I once lived in New York City and appreciate the spaciousness of California grocery stores. There are people from Manhattan who suffer a form of agoraphobia in Los Angeles markets; the open space between the aisles, the less regimented layout, and all that light are enough to disorient anyone who ever fought his way out of a Grestidies or Bohacks. But I like the larger stores. They're part of the Southern California credo that no endeavor is so modest that it doesn't deserve stage craft.

Thinking of my grandmother's attempted lunch left me craving a well made tuna sandwich. I take the simple approach: Bread, white chunky tuna packed in water, mayonnaise and you're done. Bread may be toasted and I long ago made the switch from white to wheat. White bread is not what it once was. The last time I tried it, it didn't seem to be anything at all.

I live alone in Los Angeles so most of my meals consist of variations on the pierce-film-to-vent cuisine. But I can also boil water, so I decided to treat myself: A plastic container of tortellini served with the contents of a plastic tub of pesto sauce. A bottle of white wine and some breakfast things and my shopping is complete, well within the twelve items or less limit.

The grocery store parking lot wasn't crowded, but I parked closer to the exit than the store entrance. This is one of the few pieces of advice I received from my father: Parking too close to where you're going makes it harder to get out later. I don't know how this is supposed to work, but I continue to take his word for it. He left me so little in the way of fatherly wisdom I feel obliged to heed what there is of it.

Walking across the lot with my two plastic bags I saw the blue Volvo station wagon from the house next door parked across the row and eight empty spaces down from my car. Whoever drove it there must have arrived shortly after I did. The driver was probably in the store with me. We might have passed each other in one of the aisles. I didn't remember anyone in particular in the store, but I was focused on my tuna fish and wondering why Hellman's Mayonnaise has to change its name when it crosses the Mississippi River.

I put my bags in the back seat, got behind the wheel, but didn't start the engine. Looking through the windshield and slightly to my left I could see the Volvo and for some reason it was important to know who the driver was. So, I sat in my car, waiting for the owner to come out of Vons, assuming that's where he or she was.

This was more curiosity than stalking and at least partially work avoidance, but the longer I sat there the more important it became to see who my temporary neighbor was. I reached for the copy of The Los Angeles Times I bought at the check-out and started going through the California section, cautiously approaching the editorial page. The L.A. Times has a virulent right-wing cartoonist who has never forgiven us for what we did to Richard Nixon. His idea of timely commentary is to depict Ted Kennedy as an overweight hippie shouting "Free love," an image he draws about three times a year.

Today's cartoon appeared to have something to do with traitorous celebrities. While attempting to decode it I heard the sound of a car door opening and looked up to see a woman unloading her shopping cart into the Volvo. She was in her late thirties, possibly older. She wore jeans that actually came to her waist and a dark red turtleneck under a denim jacket. Her hair was a dark mass of soft waves, gathered into a pony tail by some kind of clip or fastener at the back of her head. She had the sort of high cheekbones and full mouth I always think of as Neapolitan and associate with Sophia Loren. But this woman was thinner, more athletically shaped. She had four shopping bags to my two.

Once the bags were loaded she pushed the empty cart back to the front of the store which is something I appreciate in a person. I watched her walk back to her car, a steady, untroubled gait on boots with a fair amount of tapered heel. She gave an over the shoulder look as she was about to open the car door, a gesture of vulnerability I often see done by women alone in parking lots, opened the driver's door, tossed her small leather fold of a purse onto the passenger seat, then got into the car. A moment later and she was driving out of the parking lot, easing into traffic and heading back toward the beach.

I don't know why, but I'd expected my neighbor to be a woman and felt satisfied by the confirmation. I put the paper aside and started my car. Pulling out of the parking lot I realized if I caught up with her on the drive back it would appear that I was following her home. So I turned north out of the parking lot to take a longer way back. This meant boxing a stretch of open fields and produce stands before turning onto a road that passes a golf course and the PictSweet Mushroom Farm before leading to the access road to the Channel Islands Harbor and Marina. There I turned south, went past the power plant again and in a few minutes reached the collection of buildings that marked my turn for the pocket of vacation homes.

The Volvo was back in the driveway when I pulled in. The bags were gone from the back seat and my neighbor was nowhere in sight.

If I see her again, I'll say hello, but I don't know if I should mention seeing her in the parking lot at Vons.

After 1950, Joi Lansing could no longer depend on Metro-Goldwyn-Mayer, but she wasn't the first actress to learn the end of a studio contract could mean more work, even though that work might be in lesser pictures. In the year following her divorce from Lance Fuller she worked (uncredited) along with Kim Novack and legendary stripper Lili St. Cyr in the Howard Hughes produced *Son of Sinbad*. She appeared as a showgirl in the Jane Russell (b. 1921) musical *The French Line*, filmed in 3-D and promoted with the declaration: "J.R. in 3D! She'll knock both your eyes out!"

I saw *The French Line* as it was intended to be seen at the end of an exhaustive 3-D retrospective at The American Cinematheque in the restored Grauman's Egyptian Theater on Hollywood Boulevard, a few blocks down from the more famous Chinese. This was properly presented 3-D, shown with Polaroid glasses and double interlocked projectors, so the entire movie, except for those items thrust at you, which included trays of canapés as well as Miss Russell's chest, seems to be taking place just behind the frame. *The French Line* is probably the most torpid film ever condemned by the Catholic Board of Decency. Their big problem was one musical number in the last reel with Jane dancing around in a costume designed to take advantage of her figure and the stereoptical technology while singing about her remarkably generalized need for a man.

Joi can be glimpsed very briefly in two scenes; exiting a hotel room early in the picture and later sitting on a desk in profile at the left edge of the frame. In the second scene, you can watch Joi breathe dimensionally in a tight green dress while another character makes a call, one of the many scenes during her career in which Joi patiently waits for somebody to get off the phone.

Her performance in *The Brave One* received a backhanded compliment when the critic for *Variety* commented, "...the only cash value here is the possibility of ad and lobby art using Joi Lansing, a well filled-out blonde." Producers took this as a mandate. Joi's participation in a movie would always include a session of cheesecake photos with only the most tenuous connection to the films themselves.

One of the most effective examples of a little Joi going a long way can be found in the promotion of *Hot Cars* (United Artists, 1956). Second billed for the first time in her career, Joi appears in numerous stills, newspaper art, lobby cards and is the prominent figure on the film's rip-roaring one-sheet poster ("A stop-at-nothing Blonde...A Buck Hungry Guy...A red-hot Racket...Slam the screen head on!"). Not bad when you consider her total screen time to be about seven minutes. Proportionally this works out better for her than many of her other movies since *Hot Cars* is only fifty-eight minutes long. Made on a tight schedule and a modest budget with second-string talent in front of and behind the camera, *Hot Cars* is a second feature; a short, simple genre story intended to fill out the program.

The credits run over Joi, who plays stop-at-nothing blonde Karen Winter, taking a snappy little convertible for a test drive with the hero, Nick Dunn, an honest used car salesman played by John Bromfield (b. 1922), an actor who rarely got to play a lead and who retired to become a commercial fisherman within months of completing work on this movie.

Joi and John drive up the California Incline and into Santa Monica, pulling in at Jack's at The Beach, a restaurant built on a pier and sharing a parking lot with Pacific Park, one of the great Los Angeles movie locations of the fifties and sixties. The rides and arcades of this vulgar year-round carnival have shown up in everything from *The Beast From 20,000 Fathoms* (Warner Bros., 1953) to *The Incredibly Strange Creatures Who Stopped Living and Became Crazy Mixed-Up Zombies* (Fairway-International, 1964).

Over cocktails Nick tells Karen about the car they've been driving. She leans forward with every automotive detail, urging him on with, "I just love to be talked into things."

Returning to the used car lot Karen appears to give Nick the brush, getting into several tons of Chrysler convertible and driving off, leaving him to face the wrath of his pushy boss who's interested in volume sales and not joyrides with shapely babes.

Not that our hero is one to wander. We go home with him on his dinner break to a tidy bungalow where his wife waits dutifully in the kitchen. Theirs is a happy marriage marred only by the unexplained illness of their off-screen son.

Returning to the used car lot, Nick helps a dignified older gentleman named Markel steer clear of a lemon. That's the last straw for Nick's boss who tells him to get off the lot.

The next day Nick is starting his job search when he gets a call from Mr. Markel who's been trying to track down the honest salesman. Nick goes to Markel's office where he learns the businessman owns a chain of used car lots. He was checking up on the competition when he crossed paths with stalwart Nick. Markel offers him a job with a fat raise and sends Nick off to start work at a new lot. Nick's honesty is finally being recognized and rewarded. Now his off-stage son can get the medical help he needs.

No sooner does Nick leave the office when Markel picks up the fifteen pound bakelite rotary phone and places a call. Across town, Karen, presumably naked under a sheet, turns over in bed, her hair in place, lipstick unsmudged by sleep, and picks up her ringing telephone.

Markel thanks her for steering him in Nick's direction; he's just the sort of honest chump Markel's interstate stolen car racket needs as a front. He tells her to go out and buy that mink stole she had her eye on and be wearing it when he picks her up for dinner that night. She thanks him, referring to him as "Uncle Al," then hangs up and leans back in bed.

Nick starts at the new lot with a week's salary in advance and settles into the job of giving each customer a square deal. All around him is the pride of American car making in the fifties; wide, baronial boats with chrome grills like gnashing metal teeth, thick rudders, and V-8s standard under the hood. The sort of cars in which men felt obliged to wear a hat.

While Nick supervises the lot like a cattle boss working an automotive herd to the railhead in Kansas City, a plain clothes detective shows up with a list of hot cars stolen in the north and suspected of being shipped to Los Angeles. Nick assure the detective that nothing untoward would ever happen on one of Markel's lots. The detective, unaccustomed to someone as honest as Nick, smiles, gets into his stock Ford and drives away.

That night, Nick is left on the lot when his manager, Smiley Ward (Mark Dana, who will also appear with Joi in The Bowery Boys film Hot Shots) is called away. Nick's alone at the lot when a trailer pulls in loaded with tons of American steel; cars with swooping hood ornaments, portholes punched in their fuselages, and AM radios that needed a minute to warm up.

Hutton, the truck driver played by John Frederick under the name John Merrick, charges into the office and turns off the lot lights telling Nick that Markel likes certain deliveries made in the dark. He orders Nick, with suspiciously hep-cat jargon, to help unload the carrier. Nick complies, but he's not happy about it. The cars are driven off the truck in a brief montage sequence; bold, noir-ish compositions feature the big machines backing off the carrier, pinpoints of light kicking from their gleaming sides.

The truck driver pulls away in the clanking dinosaur skeleton of the empty car carrier and Nick, his face grim, locks the office and prepares to leave the lot. A familiar Chrysler convertible pulls up to the office. Nick looks beyond the glare of the massive headlights and sees the driver is Karen. She moves from behind the wheel to the passenger seat where she kneels throughout the scene, the closed passenger door between her and the angry Nick.

She wears a dress with a low, scooped neckline, the one in the art work on The National Enquirer issue about her attempt to win Stan Todd's heart. A diamond necklace circles her throat and drops a glittering stalactite to lead the eye to her bosom. And draped over her shoulders is the mink Markel bought her.

She hints she's been looking for Nick. He doesn't exactly believe her, but he doesn't challenge her either. Besides, he has other fish to fry at the moment.

"You've got a look that looks like trouble," she tells him, then suggests they go back to Jack's for a drink. He can tell her what's going on, maybe blow off some steam, before doing something he might regret.

There she is, all blonde and shimmering on that half-acre front seat and we know she's setting the guy up for something. She's wearing the damn mink, for crying out loud. Markel sent her for some reason, perhaps to learn how Nick is taking the discovery of what kind of dream job this really is.

She looks up at us in the artificial moonlight, smiling, promising.

"Let us go then, you and I," she seems to whisper. "To a dim black-and-white bar where we will have martinis and I will look deep into your eyes and listen to all your problems. Other men in the bar will see you talking to me and they will be jealous of you. Then, if you still want to sock somebody instead of staying with me, at least you'll have a couple of drinks under your belt."

We know more than he knows, more than he even suspects. In spite of our knowledge, we don't want him to turn her down. He should say no. He should go knock Markel's block off then go home to his wife and unseen child. But if he did, we'd feel disappointed by the decision. Why? Is it because a mink draped blond never offered us comfort or is it because we don't know what we'd do if one ever did?

Do we want Nick to go with Karen because we wouldn't go? Safe in the dark we encourage him to take the risks we refuse to take in the face of opportunities we'll never get. It's cruel in a way, as if we wanted to punish him for sins we lack the courage to commit.

After college I worked at a low wattage AM radio station on the border of New York and Pennsylvania. I sold thirty-dollar-a-spot radio commercials to local restaurants, each one a "unique dining experience," and wrote the copy which was either recorded on tape cartridges or, if it was going to be read live by the on-air personality, kept in a book with a segmented metal spine in the air studio. There was a smaller broadcast booth, a glass box facing the larger studio, where one of the three newscasters sat to deliver rip-and-read Associated Press wire copy and local school snow closings.

Two of the newscasters were relatively shapeless men, as are most of the people involved in radio. The third was a girl who looked much too good to be only a voice. Her name was Gloria. She was olive skinned and always put on fresh lipstick before she went into the booth to read the news. Her hair was heavily influenced by the 1977 remake of *A Star is Born*. She would pull it back into an auburn cloud at the base of her neck, securing it with a length of green yarn when she was in the booth. She smiled a great deal, wore blouses open at the neck and talked about the good times she had at The Rhineskeller the previous weekend.

I would try to plan my revisions of the on-air copy book to coincide with Gloria's shifts in the news booth. The on-air personality would hand off to Gloria then step back from the horseshoe shaped broadcast console. I'd take his place and pull sections of the copy book from the metal frame and update the certificates of deposit interest rates and this week's sale items at Lundy's Bed and Mattress World. Through the thick glass I could see Gloria, a huge set of earphones pushing back her hair, reading the A.P. summary of world events. Her amplified voice, robbed of echo and presence by the sound proofing of the tiny booth, came to me over the monitors in the broadcast studio. Looking at her freshly made-up lips mouthing words that came out of a speaker behind me was like watching a movie dubbed into English.

One night I was in the tape library, which was a walk-in closet at the end of a paneled corridor on the broadcast floor containing shelves of flat white boxes holding five-inch reels spooled with brown, quarter inch magnetic tape on which had been committed thousands of commercials, jingles and air checks. The room was lit by a double run of bare fluorescent tubes controlled by pulling a length of string tied to the short on-off chain of the fixture. A metal washer the size of a half-dollar was tied to the end of the string to keep it hanging straight.

I was looking for a reel of commercials I'd written and produced for Capt. Ben's Fish Dock when Gloria came into the closet. We said hello, then she turned to a shelf of air checks, running her finger along the dates written on the edge of each box with black magic marker. At least four different hands and a dozen markers could be detected in this manual labeling process. The different writing formed strata like the levels in sedimentary rock. Since these archives were one of my responsibilities, my handwriting was the current one.

The trail Gloria followed led her along one of the shelves blocked by the open closet door. So she closed it about two thirds of the way in order to reach the tapes near the hinges.

I found the box I was looking for, but kept on searching, looking over at Gloria who must have been planning to go directly to The Rhineskeller after her shift. Instead of her regular work variation of blouse and slacks, she was wearing a short, airy dress of a pale purple color. Not purple. The lighter one with more gray. Lilac.

She eliminated each box, giving it a tap of dismissal with her right index fingernail, then moved on.

At the end of the hall someone slammed into the crash bar of the fire escape door and stepped outside for a cigarette. The change in air pressure was enough to pull the closet door shut with a faint click.

Gloria turned from her box tapping and looked first at the door then at me. Above us buzzed the fluorescent tubes. At first I thought she was afraid we were locked in. We weren't. Even if we were, the push button lock in the knob of the hollow core door wouldn't be a problem. But she wasn't afraid.

"A situation in the making," she said.

I felt what I thought was a fly brush my ear, but when I lifted my hand to swat it away I found it was the washer and string attached to the light pull chain. My knock sent the washer wobbling into the air between us, the short chain clinking against the metal of the fixture. I grabbed the washer to stop it.

Then I did the most unexpected thing I've ever done. I pulled the string and turned off the lights. With the darkness came silence, the tubes stopped their buzzing.

I could see nothing of Gloria. If I'd had a plan this would have been the time to put it in motion and apparently that's what Gloria expected me to do because, after what she felt was a decent interval, I heard her voice, disembodied as it was on the radio, three feet in front of me.

"Something's going to happen or it isn't."

It wasn't a question, simply a statement.

What happened was this: I pulled the string and turned the lights back on.

Gloria was standing where she was when I turned them off. She turned back to the boxes on the shelf, found the one she was looking for, opened the door and left without another word. There was nothing to say. She had all the information she'd ever need about me.

Two pulls on a piece of string had taken care of any chance I might have ever had with her. The first tug had made a promise and the second made it clear I didn't have the courage to deliver. Better not to have pulled the string at all than to be unmanned in a closet.

One of the secret powers movies have is the ability to remind us of ourselves and our mistakes by showing us things completely unrelated to our memories, but somehow able to pluck them like a string and start them vibrating. Minor movies seem to have more of this power. Why is that? Is it because we expect so little of them? Or is it because they're so sketchy our own lives rush in to fill the empty spaces in a porous plot? It doesn't happen when we're young. Only when we're older and have collected sufficient regrets does the clubfooted dialogue fall away, leaving us with Joi's face, surrounded by darkness and mistakes.

"You've got a look that looks like trouble."

What harm is there in a drink?

We don't see them leave the lot, but on the far side of a dissolve Nick and Karen are at the bar. She listens to Nick's tale of woe, all the time sitting there in the mink that rat Markel bought her. Nick cools down, but still plans to go to Markel. He leaves and once he's gone Karen makes a phone call, presumably to Markel to tell him what to expect.

Nick confronts Markel and quits, but his timing couldn't be worse. Returning home Nick learns from his distraught wife that their off-screen son has been taken to the off-screen hospital for tests and possible surgery.

Broke and with nowhere else to go, Nick crawls back to Markel and for the sake of his sick child asks back into the racket. Markel's glad Nick is being so reasonable. Nick goes back to work fencing hot cars, making runs to Markel's chop-shop, and pulling in a lot of off the books cash. His son recovers, but remains invisible throughout the picture.

Everything's going fine, then Nick's wife finds the bankbook for the account where Nick's been stashing all the extra cash. She didn't ask where the money came from when their son was sick, but now she wants to know. Nick refuses to tell her and storms out of the house.

The state detective returns to the car lot, clearly suspicious of Markel's operations and certain Nick is hiding something. Mixed up with criminals, suspected by the police, unable to talk about any of this with his wife, what's a guy to do?

Nick picks up the phone and in the next scene is in Karen's apartment where she's mixing drinks and expressing her gratitude that the bartender at Jack's gave Nick her phone number. Nick's rationale for this visit is unconvincing and therefore speaks to his honesty; a practiced liar would come up with something much more convincing. Since Karen's a woman, he explains, she might be able to help him figure out a way to tell his wife what's going on. It's hard to imagine anyone believing this story, but Karen is a woman who has done well for herself appearing to believe the things men tell her.

Suppose your man came to you and told you he'd gotten himself in a jam? A jam there might not be a way out of?

"I'd tell him, 'I'm with you, baby, all the way,'" she says as she crosses the room in her satin lounging attire. She pulls Nick into an embrace. With Nick and Karen passionately kissing, the screen fades to black, the 1950s equivalent of three minutes of soft focus body-doubles simulating coitus.

Fade up the next morning with Nick arriving home where he's greeted in his living room by two plain clothes detectives, invited in by his wife. The state detective who was investigating the hot car racket was murdered the night before. He was last seen talking to Nick at the lot and the police would very much like to know where Nick's been all night.

Nick takes his wife into the kitchen, she just seems to feel more comfortable there, and starts to explain. He asks her patience and forgiveness and she promises they can work out their little differences once he beats the murder wrap by taking the police to the apartment of the hot blonde he spent the night with.

Nick takes one of the detectives back to the apartment in order to confirm his alibi, but when Karen answers the door she claims she's never laid eyes on Nick before.

"You're not going to buy that, are you?" he demands of the cop who asks Karen if they can step into the apartment and work things out. She lets them in.

Karen responds to Nick's story by saying, "I've been to a lot of bars. I've met a lot of men and had a lot of drinks. Some men think they know me even when they haven't had the drink."

Nick watches the detective light Karen's cigarette with a pack of matches that will in a few moments be revealed to come from Jack's. As Karen flirts with the cop Nick must be making the Markel connection. Karen is selling Nick out, but why? She has undoubtedly communicated with Markel, although we don't know if it was before Nick called her and asked to come over or after he left. If the call came before, was she told to keep Nick incommunicado while the state detective has being taken care of, or did she learn of the murder only later if at all?

In the face of Karen's denials Nick offers to describe her bedroom to the cop as proof he's been in the apartment. So Karen and the detective leave the living room, exiting through a door to the bedroom while the camera dollies past the edge of the flat to meet them on the other side. The detective stays at the foot of the bed while Karen crosses to the head where she turns back to him, hands at her side, weight on her left leg, the downstage right leg slightly forward, knee bent, back straight. There's the faintest of smiles on her lips as Nick starts to describe her boudoir, calling the description from the other room, and gets it completely wrong.

Is he lying or was he never in the room? If not, what happened after the fade to black last night? And that smile on Karen's face. She knows his description will be wrong.

Nick's description ends abruptly after mentioning a fictitious canopied bed. Responding to the silence the detective and Karen return to the living room, the camera once again passing the edge of the flat, and find Nick gone, the apartment door left open in his wake. The detective grabs the phone to call in an alert while Karen comes downstage, her back to the cop, something close to a smirk on her face as the alarm goes out. She is without remorse

With barely four minutes left of its brief running time the movie bets on momentum over logic. Hoping to locate Markel, Nick returns to the chop-shop where his boss Smiley pulls a gun on him and forces Nick to get behind the wheel of a car. Smiley gets in the passenger seat and, keeping the revolver aimed at Nick, tells him to drive toward the beach.

Sometimes the necessities of a low-budget show up on screen as jerry-rigged compromises, like the dolly past the edge of the apartment wall. But sometimes they show up as bold images. That's the case when Nick drives to the beach. Shot on a soundstage, the two actors sit in the front seat of a cut-away car, Nick in a gray suit, Smiley in a lighter gray suit. The steering wheel looms large on the lower right side of the frame, the column disappearing past our ear as we look up at the men from what must be the perspective of the dashboard cigarette lighter. The low angle is intended to block the side and rear windows, eliminating the need for rear screen projection. This economical choice produces the *Citizen Kane* of car roofs; a dark, expansive canopy over the actors. Nick keeps his hands on the foreground wheel, the bad guy balances his right hand on his left thigh, leveling the gun, which is close to the center of the frame, at Nick's midsection.

The shot was composed this way to save money and time, but the result is raw graphic energy. It is a frame full of drama, drama that works independent of story. That's the great conjurer's trick of B-movies. They made stone soup out of overworked conventions and stock characters. Artists didn't make these movies, craftsmen did. The same sort of craftsman who built cathedrals.

As the two men loom over us Nick learns his intended fate. They will drive to Jack's bar, then Nick will be taken to the beach where his suicide will be staged.

This makes no sense. For one thing, it's broad daylight which would make the fake suicide an interesting attraction for bathers and lifeguards. And why does it have to be back at Jack's? There's no time to ponder this because, approaching Jack's, they see several police cars arrive ahead of them. Detectives and uniformed cops rush into the restaurant. They're probably there to check Nick's story, but why the show of force?

Smiley cracks Nick on the head with the butt of his revolver and pulls him from behind the wheel. Taking Nick's place he makes a sharp left across the parking lot and we know why it has to be Jack's and why it has to be daylight.

The phony car is gone. Now the camera is mounted in the back seat of a real sedan, shooting between the men in the front seat while holding the ceiling and side windows, enclosing the windshield as a frame within the frame. It's a ragged shot, light pouring through the windshield silhouetting the men. The car swings across the parking lot. Ahead are the supports and swooping tracks of the Pacific Park wooden roller coaster. Smiley crashes the car at the base of the roller coaster and runs into the park with the recovered Nick on his heels.

We go back to Jack's where the police have found Markel and Karen waiting. Why do they have to be here? To help kill Nick? Surely that's the sort of thing Markel would delegate. The Karen question has answers unrelated to plot.

Karen and Markel are brought out of the restaurant in a wide shot that holds them between one of the plain clothes detectives and two uniformed cops. The group pauses in front of the restaurant long enough for the detective to tell the uniformed officers to "take 'em away." Markel and Karen exit the frame and the movie without additional comment.

Joi is wearing a tight skirt cut below the knee, a long-sleeved, turtle neck sweater and a thin black belt cinching her waist. The outfit defines every inch of her astonishing figure and this brief shot, barely ten seconds long, is the only view we get of the costume in the movie. But there was a still photographer on the location when this scene was shot. He not only caught the lineup of men in dark suits interrupted by Joi, but also shot several versions of Joi alone leaning against the hood of a Chrysler, each pose designed to accent her bullet-bra figure straining against that sweater. The pictures went into the movie's press kit along with shots of Joi in the dress she wore when she picked up Nick, the mink stole dragging on the studio floor behind her, and a close-up of her blowing on a pair of toy cars she holds in her open hands. She has to blow on them. They're Hot Cars.

The full figure shot of Joi and her grill work leaning back against the Chrysler is a powerful composition. Shot from bumper-height, the aggressive front end of the big Chrysler looming over us, Joi leans back between the midline of the hood and one headlight. At this angle her breasts exhibit a cantilever effect, the upper slope of her bosom almost parallel to the ground. She looks directly at the camera, directly at us.

Reclining on the prow of that big boat of a car she looks like a mid-fifties version of a clippership's figurehead. Imagine this black-and-white eight-by-ten thumb-tacked under glass in a lobby display case. Coming Soon!

This photograph sold a lot of tickets to a movie you never heard of.

Meanwhile, Nick chases Smiley into the amusement park and onto the Pacific Park wooden roller coaster. High above Santa Monica, as the cars rattle and shake through steep inclines and vertiginous drops, Nick and Smiley fight to the death.

This isn't some fake on a soundstage. They actually mounted cameras to the shuddering car and shot the clearly recognizable principals climbing over seats, throwing punches and struggling over the gun. They are held low in the frame which is otherwise filled with the wood skeleton of the coaster, the wickedly curved tracks, and the ocean. The unpolished rawness of the moment gives this bottom of the bill program filler a touch of Roberto Rossellini; a little *Open City* on the midway. The emotion you feel after surprise is gratitude. They went to a great deal of trouble to shoot this fight when they could have thrown together something much simpler and cheaper that would have worked just as well. After all, it's not like anybody was ever going to care about this picture.

With the detective looking on, the coaster car crests a hill and a body sails out into the California sunshine accompanied by a scream heard over the rattling of the ride. The train rolls into the station and the cop helps a bruised Nick to his feet. Nick's ready to tell everything he knows about Markel and the police are ready to listen and give him a break.

Nick and the detective exit the ride and that's the end of the picture. The video cassette I own looks like it was dubbed from a 16 mm print with plenty of damage, especially at the reel breaks. Nick and the cop are lost in a field of scratches and torn sprocket holes and the "The End" that abruptly comes on screen is clearly spliced on from another movie.

I anticipate no major restoration or two DVD collector's editions of *Hot Cars* in 2006 to celebrate its fiftieth anniversary. It is a film without significance, probably seen by more people on television in the sixties than by people in theaters during its initial release. Movies like this once filled late night hours on local channels hungry for inexpensive programming.

Those opportunities to see these films are gone now. Cable is full of more contemporary entertainment and the idea of local broadcasts is an unprofitable notion from a time when television sets had antennas. So thousands of movies like *Hot Cars* are forgotten, but not gone. They sit in vaults somewhere, carried on the books of indifferent corporations, quietly depreciating until there's nothing left except a picture of a pneumatic starlet leaning against the hood of a car long ago consumed by rust.

I decided to follow my prepackaged pasta with an extra glass of wine and a luxurious bath in Mark and David's near Roman bathroom.

Frankly, I was intimidated by the space when I saw it last night. It's huge. You could fit most of my apartment in their bathroom. The marble vanity has two sinks and runs about twelve feet along the base of a mirror that reaches to the ceiling. There's a bench and built-in hamper below more mirrors on the far wall and the actual plumbing of elimination is tucked into a corner like an embarrassing afterthought. Across the deep, reddish-brown carpet from the vanity and under a skylight is an Olympian bathtub as black and shiny as volcanic rock. An array of nozzles delivers soothing or stimulating jets of water and air from the Jacuzzi, a device named after its inventors, The Jacuzzi Brothers, immigrant engineers who came to this country to build pumps for aircraft, but found their fortune in the therapeutic benefits of swirling hot water. The head of the tub, with its cygneous gold-finished faucets and handles, is against one side of the most intimidating aspect of the room: The shower.

The shower is a six foot by fifteen foot rectangle defined on two sides by black marble. The other walls are tempered glass, one with a door of the same material. It is a double shower; two heads, two sets of controls, set far enough apart that you could sit between them with both running full blast and be able to read a newspaper in total comfort except for the humidity.

I have a problem with the shower and that problem is one of scale.

I'm used to stepping into the shower, not walking across it. The dimensions of this thing suggest purposes far beyond hygiene. Purposes I know nothing about, yet suspect my ability to perform adequately.

Standing under the spray of the inboard shower head this morning, alone and naked in that aquarium, I looked through the glass walls at my multiple reflections in the mirrors over the vanity, the mirrors on the far wall and the phantom mirrors reflected in all of them. Too many views of too many me-s, all of us moving toward that essentially cylindrical shape of middle age.

With morning pouring through the skylight, I vowed to keep my clothes on in this room during the day. The electric lights are all on dimmers (What do they *do* in here?) so I can keep them at more flattering levels at night. I'll use the tub more than the shower, making the argument that the tub in my apartment doesn't have the luxurious appeal of this dark and bubbling pool.

I started the water for the pasta while there was still gray light beyond the sliding doors to the deck. By the time I sat down to my meal it was dark outside and I switched on the yellow bug bulb on the deck to avoid having dinner with my reflection in the door.

Something about being alone in an unfamiliar house reminded me of my first few months in Los Angeles when I ate by myself in a one-bedroom apartment with no bed. I had a futon and a television that sat on top of the box it was delivered in. I owned some books and a computer, a microwave and a freezer filled with Lean Cuisine.

Not only did I eat alone, but I drank alone, especially on weekends. I'd see a movie or two on Saturday, then stop at the video store for a few more. The tapes would be watched while drinking a homemade Sangria of white wine, brandy and fruit, very sweet and fairly potent.

I'd wake early Sunday morning, pull on some clothes, get in the car and drive down Ventura Boulevard, the sun rising behind me making the run of shops and restaurants look golden and worthy. After getting the Sunday papers I'd head back, now blinded by the same sun, the glare kicking back from the windows of the same shops and restaurants. It seems to me I never saw anyone on the streets those mornings. I know that's impossible, but my memory is unpopulated. There was obviously no budget for extras at that point in my life. Absent were the nameless men and women who can briefly make a street out of a set of facades.

I wasn't lonely on those Sunday mornings. And I've never felt lonely walking on a backlot. I once walked up a hill behind the big outdoor tank at Universal, the one with a three-story mural of a perpetually blue sky, and sat on the porch of the Bates house writing postcards, looking down at the motel along the path Lila took while Sam kept Norman busy in the office. When you walk around the few remaining studio lots in Los Angeles, you feel yourself in the company of overlapping sets of ghosts, one for each movie you remember.

Perhaps I'm more ghost than they are. They still inhabit the movies. All I'll leave are postcards.

After dinner I covered the bowl of leftover pasta with plastic wrap and put it in the refrigerator. Washing the pot and one dish I could hear sounds of a television in the house of my neighbor. Nothing distinguishable, just the sense of recorded voices and music coming through the open deck door. I refilled my wine glass and headed back to the bathroom.

I stayed in the churning tub about half an hour pondering the things disposable income can buy. The hot water and wine made me syrupy with fatigue. When I climbed out of the tub I pulled on a robe, one of a pair that was hanging from a hall tree near the hamper. It was a voluminous terry-cloth thing the color of oatmeal, going down to the floor with a thick belt and a hood. I felt like a very absorbent monk.

I haunted my temporary home, going down to the first floor with my refilled wine glass and looking in the smaller bedrooms, opening closets, pulling out dresser drawers. I found a set of free weights, a wet suit, a box of unlabeled audio cassettes, a pair of Mephisto walking shoes (size 11), and a stack of *Vanity Fairs*, the most recent being the April 2001 "Legends of Hollywood" issue with a regrettably superficial article about the history of Cinerama.

When I got back upstairs I opened the deck door, but couldn't hear the television any longer. She must have turned off the set. I closed the door, turned off the lights and went to the bedroom where I unpacked my laptop and stretched out on the bed still in the robe.

I was disappointed by the bath. I'd anticipated a more Hollywood experience. The thing about fantasies is that they are rarely first person experiences. We always seem to imagine observing ourselves in the dream, a more cinematic point of view than the one we're locked into. That may be why Mark and David included so many mirrors in the bathroom and bedroom and throughout the house. It's not enough to live out a fantasy, you have to figure out some way to watch yourself doing it as well. Otherwise it doesn't count.

I turned on my computer and plugged a thin finger of metal and plastic into a port at the back. This is a digital storage device I've loaded with scans of every picture of Joi Lansing I've collected. I can open a program and flip through the pictures. There are subfolders, sorted by date and title, but I told the machine to jumble the lot of them. The early and mature pictures were mixed so Joi went back and forth through her life like a shuttlecock. A pointy sweater girl of twenty; the ripe amazon in her late thirties; leaning against the hood of that '56 Chrysler to promote *Hot Cars*; almost spilling out of her costume at the 1960 Hollywood Ballyhoo Ball; perched on a stool taking dictation from Huntz Hall and Stanley Clements; and that incredible full-length shot of her from the late sixties, standing transfixed in a white hourglass gown, her look just over and beyond us.

Taken during the Scopitone years, this is my favorite photograph of her and that's where I stopped the slide show and clicked the zoom button to get closer. I clicked it again and again, till the square mosaic of the pixels started to reveal itself at the edge of her lips and around the iris of her eyes.

Joi reconstructed out of zeros and ones.

If you wanted to own this picture or any still from a movie back in the time of my youth on Long Island, you had to go on a pilgrimage to one of a handful of shops deep in Greenwich Village where the narrow streets fold back on each other like the layers of a croissant. Behind dusty windows you'd find a counter close to the street door as if pushed forward by the inventory. Beyond the counter, ceiling high shelves receded into dimness, groaning under cardboard boxes and file cabinet drawers swollen with eight-by-ten stills and lobby cards and one-sheet posters, folded in eights.

One of the unsmiling middle-aged men who worked behind the counter, and it was always men, would look at you with undisguised contempt. I never understood why they were so sad working in these candy stores. I suppose they came to these places out of love, but fifteen years of alphabetizing and refiling in unrequited anonymity had poisoned the passion, and by then it was too late for them to leave.

You looked into red-rimmed eyes and mentioned the name of an actor or director or title and said you were interested in stills or half-sheets or any material they had. He'd look at you, correctly guessing your interest far outstripped your ability to pay for such material, then step into the labyrinth, leaving you at the counter.

On either side of you were other men and boys, never women or girls, hunched over files pulled from the catacombs, their fingers scuttling like the legs of a crab over brittle stills from silent movies long turned to vinegar and posters richly lithographed on paper thinned by age to onion skin. The only sounds were the shuffling of paper and the sigh of dust settling on everything.

A few minutes and the gray man with the red eyes returns with some of your requests, never all of them. He puts two hand-labeled files on the counter in front of you. The first contains a single oddly composed on-set shot of unknown players, the surface covered with crop marks and the circular stain of a coffee cup. The other file is a thick and ancient thing with sixty or more different eight-by-tens, all desirable, some with prices lightly penciled on the back corner. Your friend on the other side of the counter notices how quickly you start checking the prices.

You select ten, narrow that to five and splurge on three which are purchased with cash and slipped into a thin paper bag with a piece of cardboard for support then sealed with two inches of shiny cellophane tape to prevent any last minute shoplifting you might consider.

On the train home you work your finger under the tape and look at your prizes. Old black-and-white pictures of somebody the world has forgotten in a movie nobody cares about anymore. Things without value to everyone else in your life. But you know different. These photographs are tokens, talismans. Each one a tangible reminder of something intangible you once saw flickering in a dark room. Something that meant more to you than to the people around you.

In the age of eBay, do those dark village shops still exist? I can't imagine them online any more than I can imagine them hiring lovely hostesses and setting out bowls of complimentary mints.

If they're gone, what happened to the files? Who has all those pictures now?

SATURDAY

After the disappointment of the Jacuzzi, I took a chance on another shower, avoiding as many reflections as possible, toweling rapidly and getting out of the bathroom before the fog cleared from the mirrors.

Joi runs like a platinum thread through the history of television. You can follow her familiar face and pleasing outline, appearing at the edge of hundreds of programs. Working steadily in all genres, from *Mister Lucky* to *The Adventures of Ozzie and Harriet*, Joi Lansing would have been unavoidable for television viewers in the 1950s and 1960s.

I've already mentioned her distinction of being on two networks at the same time in two different half-hour anthology dramas the night of November 17, 1955. I've seen one of the two shows: *A Smattering of Bliss* presented under the *Ford Theater* banner on NBC. It's one of the three titles that come up when you enter "Joi Lansing" in the open collection database at The Museum of Radio and Television. There used to be four entries, but an appearance on *The Red Skelton Show* where she plays a dream girl in a George Appleby sketch has vanished from the collection. I don't know why.

There are two museums with identical collections, one in New York, the other in Beverly Hills. The Manhattan museum is built in the shadow of CBS corporate headquarters, five stories tall with a sandstone facade. The one in Beverly Hills is marble and glass. As horizontal as its East coast brother is vertical, it sits on the corner of Beverly Drive and Little Santa Monica like the drama department of a Midwestern college.

Individuals can view items from the open collection on the museum's second floor. This is reached by a switchback staircase along a glass wall overlooking Beverly Drive. The broad treads and shallow risers of this staircase make it impossible to climb with a normal posture. One is forced into a halting Long

John Silver sort of progress, or, at higher speeds, you lean into the job and lope upwards like a primate new to moving on its hind legs. Neither is a dignified way to go and both force you to concentrate on your feet to keep from tripping. If you want to look out at the pastels of Beverly Hills you have to stop climbing and step over to the glass.

Popular myth to the contrary, there's a good deal of pedestrian traffic in Los Angeles. Beverly Hills permits diagonal crossing where you take the hypotenuse route through the middle of the intersection instead of the time consuming drudgery of crossing on right angle legs to get where you're going. This is part of a Los Angeles obsession with short cuts.

Beverly Drive is like the main concourse of some impossibly cosmopolitan airport. All those different people in purposeful motion. You'll hear English and French and Farsi and Minnesotan. You'll see formless tourists and Playmates of the Month, the latter always much shorter than you'd expect. And there are the ancients of Beverly Hills, astonishingly old women with gloves and open umbrellas. Not umbrellas. Parasols, that glow in the flat sun. Women dusted with powder and rouge who could tell you of a time when palm trees ran down the center of Santa Monica Boulevard from here to the sea and the Red Car rattled past the backlot of 20th Century-Fox, the spires of mock cathedrals rising above the barbed wire crowning the walls, shutting off the studio as if it were a medieval city braced for invasion. The walls are gone, as is the backlot. 1930s Beverly Hills blends into the glass and cement of 1970s Century City which although younger shows its age more.

There's an anteroom in the library of the museum where you sit at one of several computer terminals set on long tables, the glowing digital impersonation of a card catalogue. You use the computers to search the database for actors, titles or other criteria. Your selections are transmitted to what I assume is a hushed, windowless space somewhere in the bowels of the building where the programs are pulled and fed to a server connected to individual viewing stations.

A volunteer escorts you into one of the viewing chambers which look like ergonomically designed telemarketing boiler rooms, all beige and calm. The walls are lined with small booths separated by partitions. At each booth, one or two burgundy chairs face a counter with headphones, controls and a small television screen. The middle of the room contains several rosettes of viewing stations, chairs and controls facing a core of small screens, spaced with snowflake geometry.

Once seated in your slice of the library you put on the headphones, punch in the code number provided for the program you've selected and wait for it to appear on the screen. It's a solitary experience for the most part. Nothing makes it through the headphones from the outside world except the occasional burst of laughter from one corner of the room or another. If you look over your shoulder you can watch the backs of the other people as they lean forward in confessional postures. Sometimes you get glimpses of what they're watching. Fuzzy kinescopes of live dramas, the cartoon palette of late sixties variety shows, dusty westerns, multi-camera sitcoms that seem to be about how quickly the cast can all sit on the couch. Young visitors watch recent programs still on the air, older visitors watch more vintage material. They sit there in segmented viewing, chairs three feet apart, their minds separated by generations.

A Smattering of Bliss is the sort of comedy that used to be described as frothy. It's the story of a married team of movie writers, Hal Venner and Loretta Erskine, played by Larry Parks (1914–1975) and Betty Garrett (b. 1919) who was also in the cast of *Take Me Out to the Ball Game* in 1949.

We meet Hal and Loretta as they put the finishing touches on a script. The writing process is dramatized as the two of them acting out the scene and dictating action and dialogue to a secretary in their cozy bungalow on an unnamed studio lot. Their banter is meant to indicate wit without ever actually achieving it. There's a strained breeziness to the whole affair beginning with the perky library music punctuating every scene.

Joi plays Inez Hamilton, the star of their latest script in production. Hal is smitten with Inez. Loretta tries to dismantle her opposition with cleverness that proves counterproductive.

This is the most all out Marilyn impression I've ever seen Joi do, pushing her voice higher and increasing its breathiness as she commits to lines such as: "The script is just frantic. You writers, I don't know how you do it. Putting down all those words so neat and together."

Inez highjacks Hal for a day at the races. Loretta is left with nothing but her sarcasm and anger at being conned into holding a party in Inez's honor. Moments later Loretta is interrupted in her office by best friend and rejected suitor Sim, played by Richard Deacon (1921–1984), who arrives with the news, "I just saw your husband take off in a convertible with a hardtop blonde." She tells him she knows all about it and talks about how much she loves the guy and how hard it is to be a smart dame in a town full of peroxide barracuda like Inez.

At Hal and Loretta's party, Inez is discovered in a sequin covered sheath reclining on a poolside chaise in beautiful black-and-white day-for-night, a process through which filters and under exposure conspire to convince you a scene shot on a short day schedule was photographed at night. It usually ends up looking like the scene took place during a lengthy solar eclipse, but done right it has the warming comfort of theatrical convention.

Inez is attended by Hal and several other men, all in tuxedos. She's talking about how the studio doesn't want her to do anything that might endanger her legs. Loretta arrives commenting if Inez broke her leg the studio might have to shoot her. Hal winces. Inez lets this roll off her satin smooth back.

Every wisecrack Loretta produces only manages to dig a deeper hole. The attacks are the reason for Hal's defense of Inez as much as his understandable attraction to this sugar cookie of a starlet who wants to do something serious on an epic scale: Inez is lobbying the studio to play Mrs. Genghis Kahn.

Loretta's actions are self-defeating. As the party progresses she literally forces her husband into the arms of this woman. Not that Inez is above taking advantage of the situation. When Hal approaches Inez for a dance, Joi opens her arms to take him in, her lips and teeth parting as if she were about to nibble him or swallow him whole.

Maybe Loretta wants the marriage to fall apart. Perhaps that's the real engine behind the sarcasm and snappy comebacks. Could it be Loretta wants out? If so, Inez offers her the best of both worlds, freedom and the saintly status of victim. Inez becomes a savior instead of a homewrecker.

"I will save you, Loretta," Inez promises as she pulls Hal into her embrace. "You won't have to make a decision, you won't have to confront him with how things have faded between you. You won't have to finally talk about how you write together more often than you make love. Step back, turn away, look brave and I will rescue you. And no one will ever know the truth except you and me."

"Inez isn't as dumb as you think," Hal tells Loretta as they argue after the party.

Rather than fight, Loretta runs, leaving for New York to help Sim with a play. Since Sim has openly stated his willingness to take Loretta on the rebound he doesn't challenge the wisdom of retiring the field to Hal and Inez. In New York, Sim confronts Loretta with news that the growing relationship between Hal and Inez has received the dubious credibility of the gossip columns. Loretta decides to fight for her man and returns to Los Angeles where she surprises Hal in Inez's dressing room working on a scene. Inez is again discovered on a chaise, now wearing what they used to call a dressing gown.

More sarcasm from Loretta and then the suggestion that they all go to dinner which they do. At dinner Loretta tries once again to destroy Inez with her bargain basement Eve Arden act, but this time Inez responds. Joi delivers something close to a monologue and puts Loretta in her place.

"Maybe I'm dumb, but at least I'm direct," she tells the writer in front of everyone at the table. "I say what's on my mind. It saves time. If there was somebody after my husband I'd tell her to lay off."

At long last speechless, Loretta leaves the table. Hal goes after his wounded wife. He's seen the error of his ways and becomes protective of Loretta who is now vulnerable in his eyes.

Sim drops by the office on his way back to New York and learns that Loretta has redirected the power of victimhood in order to regain her husband. He finds a typewritten scene containing the exchanges of dialogue he heard between Loretta and Inez at the dinner table. The reason Inez seemed so smart is because Loretta wrote the speeches for her, part of a secret negotiation. In return for her husband, Loretta promised to write Inez's vanity project about Mrs. Genghis Kahn. What's artistic integrity in the face of marital bliss?

Cleverness has won after all, but only by improving the lot of the blonde whose interest in Hal was always literary. It was the script Inez wanted, not the man who would write it. Whimsical library music informs us that all is well as Hal and Loretta exit, leaving the freshly rejected Sim holding the manuscript of Loretta's deception.

I've been unable to locate or learn any details beyond the title of the piece that was over on CBS while *A Smattering of Bliss* was shown on NBC. It was an episode of *Four Star Playhouse* called *Here Comes The Suit*. I wonder what someone would have thought if they'd flipped between the channels going from Joi the starlet to Joi as whatever she played in the other drama.

Of course in 1955, while there were far fewer channels to flip through, the actual mechanics of the act would be unrecognizable to television viewers today. It was the era of the dial, when changing from station to station meant the viewer had to leave his chair, cross the room, and manually turn a knob on the front of the set which would advance the tuner to the next preset broadcast frequency with an unambiguous thunk eloquent of the decision to move on.

Televisions of that period would have had a second knob on their cabinet face, placed to visually balance the station selector and used to turn the apparatus on and control the volume coming from the single oval speaker hidden behind a hempy fabric at the base of the set. Midway between the two knobs there was a small panel concealed behind a hinged plate bearing the insignia of the manufacturer. Opening this plate revealed several unadorned shafts identified as the controls for Brightness, Contrast, Vertical and Horizontal. These black stalks projected from the metal chassis through holes large enough for you to see the golden glow of the vacuum tubes deep within the cabinet.

Today's televisions shun the touch of humans, insisting we communicate through a smaller, intermediate god: The remote. These wands offer us options instead of controls. Pushing the correct sequence of buttons takes you deep into the nervous system of the receiver, permitting endless adjustments, some familiar, some not. Missing from the list of operations: Vertical and Horizontal.

The television, which once strained to resemble a piece of furniture, has become an implacable black aquarium like the one in Mark and David's bedroom. At thirty-six inches it feels too industrial to be in a home. When it's off the blank screen tries to reflect the room and it bothers me to see my silhouette moving like a ghost through that charcoal mirror.

I started feeling hungry around two o'clock and made a tuna salad sandwich, toasting the bread to prevent it from getting too soggy. I wrapped the sandwich in a square of aluminum foil, put it in my coat pocket and left Mark and David's house.

Back in Los Angeles there would have been steeply angled afternoon light, but here the sun never managed to burn through the low cloud cover. Weather is very discreet in Southern California. If you live in the Valley like I do, you can look east to the mountains and watch the thunderheads boil up over the desert. They crowd the sky like the clouds in a N.C. Wyeth illustration and it seems impossible they won't make it over the ridge and pour into Burbank, but they never do.

I miss the summer thunderstorms I grew up with, the kind that warned of their approach by staining the sky and everything under it a bilious green. The leaves on the maple trees turned over in anticipation and there was a breeze that became a wind, pushed ahead of the downpour. Weather in the east plays chords. Los Angeles weather hits one note at a time.

The clouds were thick and low when I reached the beach, the waves breaking a hundred yards out, reaching the shore like glistening speed bumps. The Channel Islands were gone as were the oil drilling platforms that march up the coast toward Santa Barbara.

I sat on the edge of a dune and unwrapped my sandwich.

The gray sky and greenish water made me think of Jones Beach in the winter. Oxnard is chilly and damp by California standards, but to walk along the edge of the Great South Bay in February was a test of endurance. The temperature would be in the thirties, but the wind and spray made it feel colder. No sun, the ocean angry and loud, the oversized waves throwing themselves at the shore, tearing themselves apart in the process with great roars separated by almost silent pauses. A very Nineteenth Century ocean, melodramatic and proud.

In the winter it was unrecognizable as the beach of childhood summers. In July we parked in vast lots that seemed miles from the sand and reached the beach by passing through cavernous tunnels, past a refreshment bunker selling ice cream cones designed by someone who hated children and liked to make them cry. You gave the attendant your money and were handed a pale golden cake cone with a cylindrical core-sample of ice cream wrapped in thick paper and fitted lengthwise into the cone. The trick was to unroll the ice cream from the paper without rolling it right out of the cone. The area around the stand was pockmarked with fallen ice cream, the crowd noise laced with the wailing of disappointed children.

From there it was a long trek across burning sand to reach the surf, tall and green under a sky like a blue enamel bowl. I remember it with the perspective of a ten-year-old so the scale must be all wrong. If I went back now, I'm afraid it would feel contracted and compressed.

I was just starting the second wedge of my sandwich, looking out at the Rothko of green water between gray sand and grayer sky, when the composition was interrupted by a running figure. Someone jogging along in sweater, mittens and a knit cap. The person turned in my direction and waved. Only then did I recognize the runner as my temporary neighbor.

I automatically returned the wave. Without breaking stride she turned her attention back to the sand in front of her and continued on, heading north toward the ghostly lights of the fog wrapped power plant.

Had she waved because she recognized me as her neighbor or had she waved because I was someone sitting on the beach? If she recognized me, where had she seen me? Maybe she was looking out a window when I walked to the beach. I hope she hadn't recognized me from the Vons parking lot. But if she had, she would have been more likely to call the police than wave and smile at me. And she had smiled.

I thought about jogging after her and saying a proper hello, but she was a quarter mile down the beach and chasing after her seemed as awkward as waiting for her in the parking lot. Of course, I wasn't waiting for her then. I was waiting for whoever owned the car. Still.

She softened as she ran from me, toward the haloed lights of the power plant.

The door to Bob Collins' photography studio opens and Joi enters, laughing, leading a parade of models. It's that shapely blonde again, the one with the round cheeks and proud, uplifted prow. She clicks into focus, draining light from the other girls who seem vague and unremarkable in spite of their aerodynamically spiraling bra-cups.

Certainly a major part of Joi's role as Shirley Swanson on *The Bob Cummings Show* was the "job of wearing sweaters." She was there for the hair and face and body, but she was there for a hundred and twenty-five episodes, being dependably sexy and able to toss off lines such as "Come on, Bob, it's bikini time."

It's the effortlessness of her acting in these peripheral roles that helps her stay in the memory. Other actresses would try to make a meal out of a cross and a wink. Joi is confident and comfortable, she doesn't strain as if unsure of her attributes. She also knows her way around a joke. There's a lovely double-take in the episode *Grand Dad's Old Buddy*. She and another model named Yvette, who are dueling over Bob's attentions, learn he's going to judge a beauty pageant in Palm Springs. They vow to get to the event by any means possible. Yvette, who is French and shaky with her English vernacular, says they'll get there "Even if we have to hike-hitch."

Joi gets started on her next line then, in her own version of the Bob Cummings downshift, cuts the line off in mid-word and gives Yvette a look of perfect duration before returning to face front and resume the speech. It looks simple, but it isn't. You probably wouldn't notice unless she got it wrong; snapping the line in the wrong place, anticipating the look, or not knowing when to drop back into the dialogue.

Also recurring on *The Bob Cummings Show* was Nancy Kulp (1921–1991), an actress who intersects Joi's television work at several points. Kulp made a career out of playing a sort of anti-Joi Lansing. Thin, angular, of the Margaret Hamilton school of busybodies and spinsters, her most infamous role was as the mother in *Three Faces of Eve* (20th Century-Fox, 1957) who traumatizes her daughter into multiple personalities by forcing the child to kiss her dead grandmother goodbye in her coffin.

Kulp and Lansing are both in the Orson Welles' *Fountain of Youth* pilot and *The Beverly Hillbillies*. In a 1958 broadcast of Frank Sinatra's ABC variety series they appear in a sketch apparently as two versions of the same character. I say apparently because the sketch, featuring Sinatra and Van Johnson (b. 1916), is so haphazardly staged and delivered the endeavor seems in imminent danger of disintegration.

Sinatra and Johnson appear as dueling brothers, reading their dialogue off cue cards, each with his eyes focused somewhere over the other man's shoulder. Sinatra thinks he's going to be stuck with Kulp and fobs her off on Johnson. But while Frank's back is turned Johnson pulls a switch. Kulp steps away and Joi takes her place, entering from the back of the set in a plunging halter dress to the accompaniment of saxophones, muted trumpets and wolf whistles. She doesn't slink across the stage, exaggerating her body as she walks. She enters expecting the whistles and the music as her due and stays alive as a character as the perfunctory sketch grinds on around her.

Blasé about the comedy, Sinatra did pay attention to Lansing. A year later she would have a role in the Sinatra produced *A Hole in the Head*.

What was the relationship between Lansing and Kulp? Were they polite, but impersonal coworkers? Did they like each other? Were they friends? It looks like Joi is genuinely breaking up over Kulp and Cummings in *Bob Goes Bird Watching*, but I can't tell if it's Joi laughing or Shirley Swanson.

As professionals, each would have felt unthreatened by the other since they would never have competed for the same roles. Each was making a living as the embodiment of a set of assumptions; the spinster and the sex pot.

Was Joi still living alone in that Burbank house in 1958? Stanley Todd would have been her business manager at the time, but according to the Enquirer they were not yet romantically involved.

Who were Joi's friends?

There's the suggestion in a book dedicated to the work of pin-up photographer Bernard of Hollywood of at least a nodding friendship with another minor movie blonde, Barbara Nichols. Bruno Bernard is quoted as placing a telephone call to Joi: "'I'd love you and Barbara to come meet Clark Gable and me for dinner.' She didn't believe me. Clark in his Rhett Butler voice, 'Hello, honey. We're starving, so get dressed and rush on over.' Twenty minutes later, the two blonde glamour girls arrived dressed as if they were going to the governor's ball in *Gone With The Wind*. I introduced Joi Lansing and Barbara to Clark Gable. We ordered exotic dishes at Don The Beachcombers. Clark played it cool that night. Three years later, Barbara landed a part in his production *The King and Four Queens*."

Wading through the bitchiness that is *Halliwell's Film Guide* (Seventh Edition) I found a 1956 release date for *The King and Four Queens* putting the Bruno dinner in 1953 matching up with Lansing's divorce from Lance Fuller and her move to Burbank. The twenty minutes Bruno Bernard mentions is probably an exaggeration, but it does indicate Joi was able to get in immediate contact with Nichols and coordinate the date.

If Nancy Kulp was at the opposite end of the movie female continuum from Joi, then Barbara Nichols (1929–1976, born Barbara Nickeraeur) represented a brassier, more brittle variation of the same themes of sexual availability and physical pulchritude Lansing played. Lansing, who credited Bob Cummings with sparking an interest in health food and weight lifting ("It develops the bust, cushions the hips, and slims down the waist," she told an interviewer.), radiated an alert energy. Nichols came across as just slightly over ripe. As she aged she exploited that sense of better days gone.

Lansing and Nichols are available for side by side comparison as The Coogle Sisters in *Who Was That Lady?* (Columbia Pictures, 1960). Wearing identical costumes they appear as a pair of sisters double-dating Dean Martin and Tony Curtis. It's tempting to look at their footage in the film as a fictionalized version of their date seven years earlier with Clark Gable, but the Coogles weren't as smart or successful as Lansing and Nichols who spent so many nights moving through Hollywood looking good and being seen.

I can't imagine what it's like to prepare yourself for that level of public presentation. Think of the amount of time and maintenance required to merely cross the threshold, to assemble yourself and then coldly criticize the construction. Does the mind start to lose touch with the body? When Joi looked in the mirror by the door in that Burbank house, what did she see? Did she fragment into design elements; hair, lips, breasts, never integrating into someone she recognized as self? I have trouble walking out of the house on a good day and then only by judging steeply on the curve, but to be the custodian of that face and figure. Was she ever daunted by the responsibility?

Unlike Nancy Kulp, Nichols would have gone up for the same roles as Lansing and they appeared on many of the same series. They probably met each other coming and going at auditions. Something like that could engender jealousy or a sense of camaraderie, depending on who these women were and what they wanted. Initial suspicion would have quickly faded once they realized how much they had in common.

I like the idea of these two being close, the Mormon from Salt Lake City and the former burlesque dancer from Queens. It makes both their lives seem less lonely to think each had someone they could trust and confide in, someone uniquely capable of understanding without speaking.

After a long day at their respective studios perhaps they met for drinks and girl talk.

Joi lived in Burbank so The Smoke House across the street from Warner Bros. would have been convenient. It's a place where the dark carpets are as thick as the Thousand Islands dressing, with padded booths scalloped out of the walls of the main dining room.

Living closer, Joi would arrive first, perhaps getting a head start at the bar. She would sip a martini then set it on the bar in front of her, taking a moment to study how the light passing through the gin danced on the back of her hand, her first two fingers curled around the stem of the glass, the long, China-red nails pointing back at her, the ghost of her lipstick on the rim of the glass.

She would look at the watch on her slender wrist, wonder what's keeping Barbara and sigh as the warming cold of the martini started to spread inside her. Except Joi was a Mormon and didn't drink. So, the martini was ordered for Barbara and now waits next to Joi's highball glass filled with ginger ale tinted pink by grenadine.

Horizontal sun and a blast of thick afternoon heat as the doors to the parking lot open. Joi looks past the archway and sees the distended shadow of Barbara's figure on the carpet. The doors close and Barbara enters the bar. Joi goes to her. There is that easy hugging that women do, that squeal of greeting as they briefly embrace, their bosoms pressed together by the hug. The men watch them return to the bar. Joi sips her ginger ale, Barbara lights a cigarette. Putting down her glass, Joi lifts her head and catches a man looking at her. She holds his eye the way she does the camera lens.

"Yes, I look like this. How fortunate for both of us."

Caught, the man looks away.

Barbara finishes her cigarette. They leave the bar and go into the main room for dinner. They walk side by side, their hips almost touching. The men watch the rolling of their asses as they leave and once they've gone they watch the space their asses occupied.

It's early for dinner and the dinning room is almost empty. Joi and Barbara slide into a booth. Two busboys watch from across the room as they order more drinks and debate about indulging in the garlic cheese bread. They reach a compromise, one order of the bread then each will have a chef's salad. Joi asks for her dressing on the side.

Work is discussed. They compare Jack Benny stories and fall into an unself-conscious intimacy that isolates them from the rest of the room where men look up at the sound of their laughter. The two women appear oblivious to this attention, but they must be aware of it. It fills the atmosphere, like the flecks of dust floating in the sun coming through the diamond-shaped windows, like static electricity brushing the fine hair at the back of their necks. They both sense it and when they look at each other they see acknowledgment with a thread of gratitude or possibly relief.

"They continue to look at us."

"We are good at who we are."

Dinner is finished, dessert is declined. They split the check and leave the dining room. Every man in the place watches them go, their gaze trailing after them like heat rippling the air.

After a visit to the powder room where they repair microscopic disturbances to hair and make-up, they leave the restaurant, stepping into the humid evening. Another brief embrace, their powdered cheeks brushing together, then they part.

Unlike Nichols, Joi had a hard time playing convincingly dumb. Standing near the launch pad in her single uncredited scene at the beginning of *Queen of Outer Space*, (Allied Artists, 1958) she clings to Larry, her space jockey lover, expressing her concern over his blasting off with the breathy lament that "Rockets are dangerous. They blow up."

And you just don't buy it.

Moments later disappointment in her performance is erased when the stock footage Atlas rocket, stretched to a squat fireplug of a phallus by the CinemaScope lens, lifts off. Joi looks skyward as the wash from the rocket engines hits her. The wind brushes her hair and disturbs the green chiffon of the prom dress she wears. For an instant she almost covers her bosom, shielding it from the rolling heat, but instead leans into the roaring elements like the heroine of a Victorian novel standing at land's end looking out at a wild and punishing sea.

Perhaps she's hoping Larry is near a view port, watching her as he rents the heavens.

It's a very moving image.

Standing on the deck of Mark and David's house, poking at the rest of the tuna fish, but thinking about the cheese bread at The Smoke House, I heard the front door of the house next to me open and close. I looked over the edge of the balcony.

It was after five and the lights attached to the garage had already been switched on by the timer. A wedge of shadow cut across the pavement between the two cars in the driveway, then my neighbor appeared and went to the back of the Volvo. She was dressed for an evening out. A tan coat over a gray dress that came to her knee. She'd worked on her hair, lifting it from her neck. Curly tendrils dropped from her temples and she was wearing make-up. I thought about stepping back from the edge, but I didn't think it was likely she'd look up in my direction. If she did, I'd wave and smile and say hello.

She opened the tailgate and checked something I couldn't see. Then she closed the gate, adjusted the small evening bag that was slung over her shoulder on a thin gold chain, and went around the driver's side where I lost sight of her. I heard the car door open and close and a moment later the engine started. She backed out of the driveway, already turning the wheel and came close to clipping the back fender of my car. Looking down through the windshield of the Volvo all I could see of her were her hands on the steering wheel. Her fingernails looked black through the tinted glass.

She turned the wheel, shifted and drove away from the house. I watched her car as it turned at the end of the street, not going directly onto the boulevard, but cutting into the parking lot behind MILK-LIQUOR-LOTTO. She drove around the store and out of my sight.

The sky over the ocean was a churning, slushy gray and it was getting colder. I put the cover on the unfinished tuna and went back into the house.

In 1956 and 1957 Joi worked twice with Orson Welles (1915–1985), once on a television pilot that failed to sell and again in what would be the director's last film for an American studio.

The pilot was for an anthology series to be introduced and narrated by Welles who would write the adaptations as well as direct. *The Fountain of Youth*, from the story *Youth from Vienna* by John Collier, was the tale told in the pilot. Set in 1922 it's the story of an older doctor who falls in love with a young actress only to have her wooed away from him by a dashing tennis player. The doctor bows out, gracefully it appears, and goes to Europe to work on his endocrinology research. He returns with a wedding gift: A single dose of an elixir that will bestow perpetual youth and essential immortality. Only two doses of the fountain of youth were prepared. The doctor has taken one, the other he gives to the woman he loves and her husband. They can't split it between them. It must all be taken or the formula will do nothing and there's only enough for one. His gift delivered, the doctor withdraws to see what happens.

Joi plays the actress, Caroline Coats, first seen by the doctor in a play titled *Destiny's Jot*. Described in Welles' narration as "One of those creatures who stands for something greater than talent, greater than beauty," Joi plays the insecurity behind vanity, giving a glimpse of what she might have done if anyone had ever asked her to do more than stand around and breathe. Shot between the eighth and eleventh of May in 1956, the short would not be broadcast until September 16, 1958.

Between the production and broadcast of *The Fountain of Youth*, Joi worked with Welles again, appearing in the opening shot of the director's last studio film, *Touch of Evil* produced between February and April of 1957.

Decades before steadi-cams and remote cranes Welles pushed the limits of the available equipment and designed the film to open with a single bravura shot lasting just over three minutes and covering several blocks of Venice, California standing in for Tijuana, Mexico. On screen during most of this shot made in the predawn hours of March 14, 1957 is Joi Lansing. But you never get a really good look at her.

Black-and-white night in Tijuana. We're at eye level, looking down as a man turns toward us, filling the frame with the crude homemade bomb he cradles in his hands: A white plastic oven timer attached to coils of wire leading to a bundle of dynamite and flashlight batteries. He sets the timer for three minutes and it begins to click.

A woman laughs.

The man turns to his left, the camera quickly panning off him in the same direction to look down a run of grimy Tijuana street. Back there, past a liquor store and under the arches of the street's overhanging balconies, we see a man and woman coming toward us. He's thick and wears a suit, she's a blonde in a long black cocktail dress and shawl.

They turn into an alley before we get a good look at them.

The man with the bomb crosses the frame from left to right. We chase him, watching his shadow rush along a wall covered with the tattered remains of posters for strip shows and wrestling matches.

Past the wall the man crouches down behind a white Chrysler New Yorker convertible parked with the top down, the trunk toward us. He opens the trunk, slips the bomb inside then runs off as the camera approaches the car and booms up high to look down as the man and woman emerge from the alley and cross to the convertible.

He gets behind the wheel, she tosses herself into the front passenger seat. He starts the car and the mix of night sounds spilling from the bars and clubs is overwhelmed for a moment by jazz from the car's radio. He puts the car in gear and pulls into the alley they just walked through. The camera, still high, loses them as it slides along the humped tarpaper roof of the building.

The camera starts to drop as the convertible exits the alley, turns into the street and starts toward us. We back over the head of a cop who stops the convertible to let the cross traffic pass. We keep moving, opening the distance between us and the couple in the convertible. People dash through the crosswalk, noises and music drown out the convertible's radio. It's a dark place, more shadow than light. Turn the wrong corner here and you couldn't be farther from human warmth and rescue if you were on the dark side of the moon.

We're half a block along when the traffic cop lets the convertible through and it charges toward us as if trying to catch up, bringing its radio music with it.

Another policeman stops the car at the next intersection and we move ahead again, this time gaining altitude as another couple crosses right to left in the crosswalk. We drop down to intercept Janet Leigh (1927–2004) and Charlton Heston (b. 1924). Janet is in sweater and skirt, Heston is in a suit and looks like he's corked up for an amateur production of *Othello*. We will shortly learn this is not a skin condition: Heston is supposed to be a Mexican prosecuting attorney, Ramon Miquel "Mike" Vargas.

Janet and Charlton look back as the convertible turns onto their street and passes them. This is the closest we've been to the people in the car and if you knew in advance it was Joi Lansing you might recognize her. Maybe you'd register those cheeks, but otherwise she's a blur.

The convertible clears the frame and we're looking back at Chuck and Janet at the center of the frame. They move toward us, coming farther out into the street to get around the convertible stopped ahead of them. We can't really see the faces of the people in the car; the top of the windshield is like a bar at face level. Joi is further blocked by the rear view mirror. She waves at something to get out of their way. The man stands up in the driver's seat. Chuck and Janet laugh. They take us in front of the convertible where we see the road block consists of half a dozen goats being taken across the street by a farmer. Behind Chuck and Janet the convertible tries to pull around the goats. It's blocked by more cross traffic and pedestrians, but eventually gets through the intersection.

We're in the border crossing area now. Chuck and Janet move downstage right, the convertible goes upstage left around a guard kiosk. On the other side of the kiosk the couple and the big car are parallel, Janet and Chuck walking even with the convertible's headlights.

They reach a check point. Janet and Chuck are questioned by a downstage right immigration officer. The people in the convertible are impatient to get through; they don't understand why this guy covered with shoe polish is getting special treatment.

You can recognize Joi as Joi now even though the shadow of the windshield frame is across her eyes. As she was for so much of her career, she is at the extreme edge of the frame while attention is focused mid-foreground right where we learn Janet and Chuck are married, that she's an American and he's a hotshot and incorruptible prosecutor.

The driver of the convertible asks, "Can I get through?"

Chuck moves to the far side of the convertible, talking across Joi and the driver to the officer about the big case he just cracked. During this, Joi looks at the hunky albeit discolored Heston, giving him the once over, the fingers of her right hand resting lightly on her bare shoulder.

When Heston and Leigh start to exit the shot, first walking back, becoming smaller elements of the composition, Joi touches her forehead.

"Hey," she says.

"You an American citizen, miss?" the officer asks.

"I've got this ticking," she tells him. "No, really, this ticking noise in my head."

The guards pass the convertible through. It wipes from right to left leaving us with a couple of uniformed immigration officers walking toward us and, deep in the shot, Heston and Leigh walking into America, right to left. The camera pushes toward them. We stop when they stop, Chuck turning Janet and embracing her in what has become a loose two-shot. He kisses her.

Three minutes have elapsed.

There's an explosion and flash of light off camera. The shot ends with a cut to a burning car dropping into frame and hitting the pavement.

The story then unfolds as an investigation into the murder not of Joi, but of the man behind the wheel, Mr. Blaine (Phil Harvey). The crime itself is eclipsed by the confrontation between Heston and rule-bending bad cop Detective Hank Quinlan played by Welles wearing the latest in a series of increasingly complicated fake noses.

There's another fleeting glimpse of Joi about ten minutes later in the picture. We know at this point that the blonde in the car was a stripper named Zita performing in town. Heston is lured into an alley outside a strip club. He stops in front of a poster for Zita's appearance. Someone throws a bottle of acid. Heston blocks the throw and the stuff splashes on the poster, obliterating Joi for the second time in the movie.

When the studio looked at the three minute opening shot with its wide angles of half-empty streets they came to the not unreasonable conclusion that it was intended as background for the credits. But Welles wanted the shot to run without titles, a wish that would go unhonored until 1998 when the film was restored and re-cut to reflect something closer to the director's intentions.

In its original release *Touch of Evil* sank like a stone. The last studio film Orson Welles would ever make quietly disappeared from theaters. By the time I showed a credit covered print in college in the early seventies it had started to acquire its current reputation.

When I went to college in Albany, I lost my amateur status as a moviegoer. I got to hold the two-thousand foot reels of 16 mm film, thread them into a pair of Graphflex projectors, turn the lights down in the lecture halls and offer these gifts to my fellow students.

For better or worse, this was when movies became "important," and my approach to them shifted from affectionate to reverential. They became precious things with the power to make me a better, wiser person. Perhaps all the power they had came from me, but it was still power. I was certain, though I never said it out loud, that if you saw the right movies in the right order, the combined alchemy of the experience would open your mind and ennoble your heart.

In my passion and innocence I worshipped films no twenty-year-old could comprehend. No one under forty can begin to understand what's going on in *Wild Strawberries*, but I knew there was something there to understand. I felt like a child eavesdropping on adult conversations I longed to join. I don't sense that longing from the people around me in movie theaters today. All I get from them now are jittery waves of whiny impatience.

I own a DVD of Jean Renoir's *Rules of the Game*. I went online, ordered it and it came to my home. I can slide it into my laptop computer and watch it anywhere, anytime I want.

Thirty-five years ago, the first time I saw *Rules of the Game*, on a double-bill with *Grand Illusion*, I had to leave my parents' house, walk to the train station, buy a ticket, catch a train, change to a different train in Jamaica, Queens, transfer to a subway at Penn Station and go downtown to an old revival house that smelled like a damp basement.

There I sat in the dark as the movie was projected on a screen substantially bigger than my laptop. And it was a projected image, light thrown through transparencies and bounced back to my eye, not a t.v. or computer screen which are themselves light sources.

Until 1979 and the first home VCRs you didn't get to own a movie. You got to see it and all you could keep was the effect it had on you. That was the contract made when you bought your ticket, the bargain struck as the house lights went down.

"I will have to pay attention and remember this."

When you're young, the movies you see and the circumstances under which you see them are vital to the kind of adult you'll become. That's why I worry about the future every time I drive past a multiplex. I passed one on the drive

hteen screen complex near a nest of factory stores. It's a grim
...g into one of those places. Movie theater lobbies used to look
...c tne antechambers of palaces and temples. Now they look like airport terminals with glass walls, crisscrossing escalators and bored security guards.

Newer theaters reverse the spatial experience of going to the movies. It used
to be you moved through increasingly larger spaces until you entered the audi-
torium which would open all around you. Now, as you move from ticket window to concession stand to departure gate, you are being squeezed into ever
smaller environments until you reach the shabby little box where the movie
will be presented. Sound from the adjacent cubes pounds the walls as you
watch out-of-focus advertising slides and savor the aroma of nachos. You're
emotionally numb by the time the trailers start. Depending on the chain and
the time of year you might get a half dozen of the things, all cut like car commercials or video games, each indistinguishable from the one before. By the
time the feature starts your numbness has deepened to a protective cocoon.
More and more people put up with this abuse, because more and more people
have forgotten, or never knew, how it's supposed to be.

The theatrical release of a new movie has devolved into a marketing device
to drum up interest in owning the reduced experience of a tape or DVD. The
people who make the movies design them for this reduction. That's why DVDs
contain so many qualifiers and commentaries, extras, alternatives and amplifi-
cations. It's an attempt to compensate for something that's missing. What's
missing is the demand that we make an effort, that we earn the right to understand what we're seeing.

Mine is the last generation that was aware there was something beyond our
grasp. There were movies, books and television shows we loved, but there was
also the sense of something else, something beyond, something we weren't
quite ready for, but if we made an effort, if we matured, we would some day
understand these richer things that whirled with complexity just over the hill.
We could see their lights reflected on the underside of the low clouds, like the
glow of the best carnival ever.

That complexity is gone now. Effort, discipline, patience, humble progression toward a desired goal; all the grown-up attributes have fallen out of favor
along with the very concept of "growing-up" as a reasonable aspiration. There
is no need to move if everything is brought to you. The hill has been leveled
and we can see that the glow isn't a carnival, but the sodium glare from the
lights of a Wal-Mart parking lot.

I know all this sounds like generational chauvinism, but it isn't. At least not all of it. I'm really not advocating bringing anything back, because I know you can't. We better hope the new forms can take on emotional resonance, because when we who remember the things that are gone are gone, there'll be no one left who knows the difference between a letter that reads "It seems such a waste to see lovely things and not be with you," and an email that states "I ms U 2 :(" or that the difference matters.

Perhaps email will replace the love letter and the blog will take over for the journal. It would be nice, but I'm skeptical. It's like trying to explain the concept of the B-side to someone who's never played a record.

The sound of a CD is crisp and clear and dynamic, creating music through the pristine logic of digital technology. It does not remember, it samples. Gone forever is the thick pah-thump of a needle dropping onto a rotating disk, picking up the groove and going for a ride while we sit in a room listening. Because there is too much to do, too many distractions, not enough time. If we stop and listen, we'll never catch up.

I poured a glass of wine and went out onto the deck. It was after ten-thirty and the Volvo still wasn't back. My neighbor must have gone on somewhere after dinner.

Throughout 1959 Joi moved back and forth between television shows, including an appearance as Miss Low Neck on *The Lucy-Desi Comedy Hour*, and feature films. She was an uncredited checkroom girl in *It Started With a Kiss* back at her old studio, M.G.M. and is one of only two women appearing in the low-budget science fiction second-feature *The Atomic Submarine*.

The best thing about *The Atomic Submarine* is the one-sheet executed by Reynold Brown, the man responsible for some of the best movie posters ever created. A former aeronautical illustrator, Brown filled *The Atomic Submarine* art with thrusting submarines battling flying saucers beneath arctic ice flows. If the movie had a fraction of the poster's verisimilitude it would have been spectacular. Instead it's filled with second-string leading men and dry-for-wet underwater effects which appear to use those baking soda powered submarines that once came in cereal boxes.

The aspirations of this Allied Artist quickie far outstrip its resources, and yet it scared me as a child. Mostly because of its whooping "electro-sonic" score and a nerve wrackingly economical use of darkness in a climactic scene aboard a sunken flying saucer. Unable to convincingly fill the space ship with anything, the filmmakers fill it with darkness, turning it into a threatening void.

The film also has one of the most annoying narrators in the history of American cinema. In an effort to pump up the general torpor of the picture, this unctuous commentary coats nearly every scene with a thick syrup of adjectives and adverbs.

And it has Joi Lansing. Just barely. She's fourth billed and appears in a single scene intended to certify the heterosexuality of the film's hero, Commander "Reef" Holloway, played by science fiction stalwart, but not especially sexy Arthur Franz (b. 1920).

Set in the near future, which in 1959 would have been 1970, the film starts with a whacking great load of exposition, narration, stock footage, bad miniatures, and that disturbing music, outlining a crisis gripping the North Pole where a mysterious force has been destroying any and all who dare trespass above the arctic circle. The killer sub Tiger Shark will be dispatched to locate and destroy this unknown phenomenon.

We go from a conference room in the Pentagon decorated with a map of the solar system identical to the one on my childhood bedroom wall I got for buying a pair of U.S. Keds, to the bachelor apartment of the Tiger Shark's executive officer: "Reef" Holloway. There we find, in the words of Orville H. Hampton's screenplay, "Julie perched on the arm of an overstuffed chair, in all her lush female magnificence—contoured and accoutered elegantly—with fine legs, long and sexy. Julie is drool-bait…"

That's the description Joi read in her copy of the revised shooting script dated May 26, 1959. That was the literary foundation on which she was to build her character. It can't have been that different from the description of every other part in every other picture she worked in or auditioned for. Almost two decades of finding yourself playing characters whose breast size is noted in the text.

Joi/Julie is smiling as she listens to Cmdr. Holloway's drunken navigation and firing officer Lieutenant Dave Milburn who stands, unsteadily, between his wife Helen and Reef. Dave is trying to warn Julie about what a dog Cmdr. Holloway is. Reef implores his friend's wife to get the drunk out of the apartment so he can try to have sex with Julie. Helen obliges saying, "I am the mother of your three children. Now take me home." The three children are wedged in here not to help the scene, but in an attempt to make us feel bad an hour from now when Dave meets his fate under the ice. By that time we will have completely forgotten the reference.

Julie watches not from an arm chair as scripted, but from the couch. She wears a dark cocktail dress, thin straps rising from her cleavage to rest on her otherwise bare shoulders. They don't appear to be loadbaring straps.

Reef gets his drunken friend and wife out of the apartment and snuggles with Julie on the couch. There's an intense kiss after which the Mormon actress lights a cigarette and takes a rather post-coital drag. She offers the cigarette to Reef.

Reef tells Julie how he might be called away at any minute on another "save the world" mission. She's heard this line before and prompts Reef, predicting his "We may only have this one night" routine. Reef looks nailed, but, what the heck, she kisses him anyway.

Reef is rounding what passed for second base in fifties movies when there's a knock and an official looking envelope is slipped under the door. Reef leaves Julie on the sofa, picks up the envelope, opens it and starts to read the orders that will send him on another damn save the world mission. Reef looks at Julie and moans.

And that's a wrap for Miss Lansing. She's finished on the picture and on to something else after what was probably about three hours work to get the seven shots that make up the three minute scene.

As kids we were glad to have the kissing scene over so we could get on to the submarines and flying saucers, but now I wish they'd taken Julie along, somehow stowed her away in a torpedo tube or something. She would have been more fun than the red-baiting Reef going after a scientist who questions the need for nuclear weapons, or the jargon laden dialogue from Tom Conway (1904–1967), the forties B-movie version of George Sanders who actually was George Sanders' brother. Conway's Sir Ian Hunt says "incredible" and "fantastic" almost as often as the ubiquitous narrator. Unlike the narrator, Conway appears to be a little drunk. Similar slurring can be found in Conway's scenes with Joi's first husband Lance Fuller in the 1956 American-International film *The She-Creature*.

The movie lumbers on, Joi-less, eventually arriving at the sequence in the submerged flying saucer, a dark limbo of contracting iris portals and sharply angled expressionistic walkways that sent me ducking behind the seat-back in front of me when I was eight-years-old. Hidden down there I never saw the unconvincing monocular octopus of an alien, but I did hear it and it sounded just like the narrator.

Reef escapes the flying saucer leaving behind the charred remains of his friend and father of three Lt. Dave Milburn, a loss that has no visible effect on the Commander and leads me to wonder how close they really were.

The Tiger Shark destroys the saucer as it attempts to flee back to its home planet with a favorable colonization report. A missile is fired and the saucer explodes in a ball of fire which is the same piece of Air Force stock footage of an aborted Atlas rocket Godfrey Reggio used as the penultimate image in *Koyaanisqatsi* (Institute for Regional Education, 1983).

The seat-back I was hiding behind was in The Cascade Theater on Post Avenue, the main street of the town where I grew up. From my first awareness until the day I went away to college, I lived with my mother and father in a Cape Cod up the block from The Cascade. I could see its red brick backside from my front steps. It was built as a legitimate theater with fly space and a backstage area. There was an orchestra pit, a loge, which cost fifteen cents extra, and a balcony I never got to see.

It was so close to home I could get there by crossing the one street directly in front of our house, so I was allowed to go to the movies on my own at an early age. At least to matinees. For evening performances an adult had to be drafted.

The design was a sort of Moorish-Tudor blend with cream colored walls, red carpets and thick padded doors covered with leather that must have started out red, but after decades of patrons was closer to the color of wine when I knew it. The Cascade had a heavy red curtain that parted to reveal a screen set just behind a proscenium guarded on each side by faux boxes decorated with scenes of lush gardens. Underneath the box stage left was a neon clock that glowed an aquatic blue during the show.

The chandelier at the center of the domed ceiling was removed in the eighties when the theater was sliced into two lopsided auditoria by a featureless wall. They didn't adjust the arc of the seats when they put in the wall so the two spaces felt off-balance. Depending which side you were on you sensed a dark, disorienting bulk at your left or right, tugging at your equilibrium. It was as if the theater had suffered a massive stroke and was now withered and blinded on one side.

It was a cruel thing to do to the place where I went from *Have Rocket Will Travel* to *Barbarella*, and where my father once covered my eyes with his warm hand to shield me from the scary parts of *The 4-D Man*.

It was at The Cascade in 1959 that I saw Joi Lansing in *A Hole in the Head*, directed by Frank Capra (1897–1991), as half of a monumental double-bill with Billy Wilder's *Some Like It Hot*. The two films have a combined running time of just under four and a half hours.

As the blacklist took root in the movie business during the fifties, Frank Capra tried to protect his career by distancing himself from the more progressive themes of his best work. This meant cutting himself off from all the screenwriters who were responsible for so much of "The Capra Touch." Capra went so far as to secretly name several writers as communists including Sidney Buchman (1902–1975), the credited author of *Mr. Smith Goes to Washington* (Columbia Pictures, 1939). Capra learned too late that when it comes to Hollywood, the compromising of one's conscience is not so devastating as the loss of good writers. *A Hole in the Head* stands in testimony to that fatal choice.

Before I went back to look at it for this project all I remembered of *A Hole in the Head* were its colors, deeply saturated and streaking across the CinemaScope screen in contrast to the crisp grays of the Wilder movie. I also remembered a distraught boy weeping as he runs out into the glare of headlights on a busy street where he is struck by a car.

The boy, the crying, the running and the street are all there, but there's no traffic accident. I'd turned wishful thinking into memory. I must have wanted the adorable, freckle sprayed, redheaded son of Frank Sinatra's widower character Tony to be injured in the twin hopes of silencing the whimsy and seeing something, anything happen in this movie.

Joi is billed seventh in *A Hole in the Head* and shows up in the movie just after the credits. We see her in a framed picture on the wall of Frank Sinatra's The Garden of Eden Hotel, a second rate establishment on a less fashionable stretch of Miami Beach. In the photo she looks longingly at Keenan Wynn (1916–1986), Sinatra's successful war buddy, as the couple board a plane.

Sinatra's Tony is possessed by the idea of building a second Disneyland in Florida. In this mad scheme he is rebuffed by one and all. He lives with his young son played by Eddie Hodges (b. 1947) who does adorable things to help his father, such as refilling his cigarette lighter and testing the flints. Meant to be an American dreamer, Tony comes across as a manipulative loser. By the end of the film he will reject free-spirited, bongo-playing, sexually available, kooky Carolyn Jones (1929–1983) in favor of emotionally distant widow Eleanor Parker (b. 1922) who tells Sinatra the story of seeing her young son and husband drown with a sociopathic blandness. This emotionless memory is told in a wide two-shot that keeps the characters at a distance from each other and the audience. Parker has her back to Sinatra when she tells him, removing even eye contact from the scene.

This was Capra's first film in the wide-screen format CinemaScope and he seems completely befuddled by what to do with the larger image. His camera hangs back, turning the frame into a puppet theater. Actors line up at imaginary footlights and play their scenes in sets that look like displays in a furniture store.

Joi rides into *A Hole in the Head* alongside Keenan Wynn in an open limo behind a police escort welcoming the big shot developer to Miami. In the car with Keenan who may be her husband, boyfriend, or employer, the relationship is never articulated, Joi wears a white and silver turban and a low cut purple dress designed by Edith Head. She is dripping with diamonds as she brushes the ashes of Keenan's cigar from her bosom.

The motorcade rumbles past Sinatra's fading hotel and is gone.

The singer undoubtedly remembered her from the sketch in his variety show the previous year. You couldn't stand that close to Joi Lansing and forget the experience. She could not have appeared in the film without his blessing, but did he suggest her for the role or simply approve her?

The film crawls forward, one turgid domestic scene after another. It seems to be about Sinatra's fitness as a father; living in this hotel with his son, ducking creditors and taking care of eccentric guests doesn't seem a proper way to raise the boy. Hovering above the action is the specter of Sinatra's brother played by Edward G. Robinson (1893–1973), a successful businessman who has reached the end of his rope when it comes to lending Tony money to keep him afloat. There's the boy to think about. Maybe he'd be better off with Robinson instead of his dreamer of a dad.

Just short of halfway into the movie we arrive at Sinatra and Hodges performing what would become the Academy Award winning song for that year, the ruthlessly optimistic and metaphorically foggy *High Hopes* which went on to become an early anthem for John Fitzgerald Kennedy's presidential campaign before it was dropped because of the feared unsavory connection with Sinatra.

We are a soul trying hour and thirty-seven minutes into the movie when Sinatra finally gets his meeting with old pal Keenan Wynn at the Fontainebleau Hotel. His plan is to get his developer friend to bankroll the Florida Disneyland project thus proving his fitness as a father.

Wynn's character has taken over the entire hotel for a loud and lavish party and Sinatra, with his roll of blueprints, is like a minor petitioner seeking favor from a Sun King who wears Bermuda shorts. There is much backslapping and "How are you old buddy?" but Sinatra's efforts to turn this into a business meeting only succeed in showing how desperate he is.

Joi is at the party in a dress the color of champagne, diamonds at her heart and wrists. She is luminously lit for Technicolor by William Daniels (1901–1970), the photographer of many of Frank Sinatra's feature films. The light finds her skin and platinum hair, the diamonds at her bosom. She is again a beautiful beacon in a Sargasso of bad filmmaking. Charging in and out of the conversation between Sinatra and Wynn, she seems to run the latter's life, telling him how late they are and how he simply must get changed so they can leave for the dog track.

Sinatra accompanies Wynn and Lansing to the dog track where they sit in the front row of a box. When *A Hole in the Head* reached television, Joi became a disembodied voice during this sequence. Glowing at the extreme right of the CinemaScope frame she is only visible in the letterboxed DVD version. On television she is banished into pan-and-scan exile.

The relationship between the width and the height of a projected motion picture image is expressed as the aspect ratio and for the first half-century of movie making that ratio was 1.33 to 1. While the history of cinema is filled with experimental ratios and film gauges, the threat of television in the early fifties is most often cited as the impetus for studios to embrace wider images, along with color and stereophonic sound, offering the audience something they couldn't get on their sets at home. The aspect ratio of movies has been getting steadily wider since the mid-fifties, moving through an extended period of 1.66:1 and settling, at least for the moment, at 1.85:1.

CinemaScope initially stretched things out to 2.55:1, responding to Cinerama's 2.77:1. It has retracted slightly. Take a dollar bill out of your pocket and you're looking at a widescreen image; American money and CinemaScope both come in at about 2.35:1.

Theaters were once gutted and redesigned to accommodate the wider images, but now multiplexes defeat the entire purpose of making a widescreen movie. With real estate at a premium and theater size shrinking, instead of pulling out the sides of the screen to make room for a larger image, they drop the top, maintaining the wider ratio, but giving it to you on a smaller screen.

During one race Joi stands while Wynn and Sinatra stay in their seats talking about the proposed real estate deal. She stands, but the camera doesn't adjust to hold her. The static composition remains the same and her head disappears above the upper frameline as she cheers on her dog, her cleavage centered in the frame.

There's an impulse to try to make this seem cruel and humiliating, but that's as implausibly melodramatic as the plot of the picture. Eleanor Parker might have balked at having her head cut off while giving the speech about watching her family perish, a staging that would have made the scene marginally interesting, but Parker wasn't hired for her body. Joi was and she knew it.

Sinatra bets on a race in which he wins enough money to save his hotel and his son without help from his moralizing brother. But Wynn urges him to let it ride. Sinatra does and loses everything on the next race. Wynn and Joi watch a desperate Sinatra root for his losing dog, their expressions swinging from surprise to embarrassment.

They brush past the beaten man on their way to their next social engagement. Sinatra chases after his old pal. What about the Floridian Disneyland? Wynn says it's a great idea. For Walt Disney. Old pal Wynn tells his friend he doesn't like being scammed. He had no intention of investing in the idea. Then why bring Sinatra to the dog track? Just for the sadistic pleasure of humiliating him?

Sinatra pleads with Wynn, reaching for his old buddy's arm. That's when Wynn's bodyguards grab Sinatra and start pummeling him. Wynn tells his goons to go easy. After all, this is an old friend.

Then Wynn, Joi and the bodyguards sink out of the movie on an escalator while a beaten Sinatra stumbles into the men's room. Sinatra returns to the hotel a dismal failure. He tells his brother to take his son and give him the decent life he can't.

The next morning tear-streaked Eddie Hodges breaks free of the brother and runs to his father who stands on the beach looking out to sea. And for some reason everything is now all right. Eleanor Parker literally steps out from behind a tree to say she'll marry Sinatra and use her money to keep the hotel going. Big brother Robinson inexplicably now sees his brother as a loving parent and okay fellow.

So, while a chorus reprises *High Hopes*, they all walk down the empty beach and into the sunset. On the east coast. At eleven o'clock in the morning.

If that double-bill started at 7:30 P.M. it would have been close to midnight when my family left the theater and walked the half-block to our house.

The Cascade had no parking lot so patrons parked their cars along both sides of the one-way street. In the summer, when I slept with the front window of my bedroom open, I'd wake at ten or eleven each night, when the last show let out, to the sound of shoes scuffing on the sidewalk, fragments of conversation, the opening and closing of heavy car doors, engines starting and cars pulling away. The ceiling of my room would fill with the overlapping triangles of headlights arcing above me like searchlights. There would be several minutes of this, more on Friday and Saturday nights than the rest of the week. Then the last car door was slammed, the final date ended and the street would be quiet again.

The clarity of those remembered nights startles me. They are recalled so sharply, so longingly, that I believe they hold some important, but deeply coded content. Like a lovely song in a language I don't understand, I'm left with the beauty of the thing, but have no sense of its meaning.

SUNDAY

Something woke me. A noise, I think, but it had stopped by the time I was conscious enough to look over at the clock on the VCR and see that it was after three in the morning.

I got out of bed, pulled on the oatmeal robe and walked into the kitchen. Street light spilled in through the second floor windows outlining the sheet covered living room furniture. I went out on the deck and looked over the edge to the driveway. The Volvo had not returned.

Was someone breaking into my neighbor's house? I put on my sneakers without bothering with socks, dropped the keys in the pocket of the robe and stepped out of the house, going to the gate then out into the driveway.

Standing in the driveway, I looked at the house next door. No visible signs of entry, no furtive vectoring of flashlight beams behind the drawn curtains. Everything seemed in order. But what had I thought I heard?

I walked backwards from the driveway into the silent street, trying to get a look at the glass door of the balcony on the other house. The back of my shoe hit something that boomed like a drum. I'd backed all the way across the street and kicked one of the recycling bins waiting at the opposite curb. I turned to the dark house behind me, trying to remember if there was anyone in it and worrying that they might have heard me.

The windows remained dark. All the houses were dark around me. There was plenty of light from the utility poles and the floodlights everyone had mounted over their garage doors. Enough light to erase the stars, but the houses themselves, those windows were all black with sleep or absence.

The ocean rolled beyond the row of houses. I could just make out the rhythm of the waves like a muffled heartbeat. Cold wind on my legs, blowing up under the robe. It felt somehow forbidden. There was an undefined giddiness, as bracing as the cold. I was up past my bedtime and outside without proper attire. There was a berserk impulse to open my robe and flash the dark houses for no reason other than I could. I pushed my hands deep into the pockets of the robe to fight the urge.

Then I heard a car engine above the ocean drone and turned to see a pair of headlights coming around from the convenience store. I could have run across the street, made a dash for the gate, but instead I took another three steps backward, past the recycling bin and into the shadows under someone else's balcony. Better to let them pass than to scamper through their headlights like a rabbit.

So I was hidden when the blue Volvo pulled into the driveway and stopped at an angle, almost against the front fender of my car. The engine was turned off, but the brake lights stayed on. I could see she was alone in the car, fumbling for something on the front seat next to her. The brake lights went out and I pressed myself into the corner where the garage door met the wall.

The driver's door opened and she swung out one stockinged leg, planting her shoe on the pavement. Nothing happened for a moment. The dome light had come on when she opened the door and I could see her hair was down on the right side. She shifted behind the wheel and put her other high-heeled foot on the cement. Her right hand felt along the ledge of the door and she leaned forward using inertia to get out of the car and stand. She stood in the driveway, leaning on the car door as if growing accustom to an unfamiliar and fluctuating gravity.

Even from across the street I know the difference between sick and drunk and my neighbor was drunk as she stood by her car marshaling herself for the treacherous trip to her front door. The chain of her evening bag was looped around her left wrist and the bag dragged behind her as she moved around the car door and used her weight to shut it. She stumbled as the door abandoned her, shutting with a click, but not shutting all the way. The dome light stayed on.

My neighbor reached out and went from hood to garage door to gate, clutching her keys in her outstretched hand. If she had fallen I would have moved to help, but she didn't fall. There was a dicey moment at the gate when she dropped her keys. She looked down, unsure how to retrieve them. Then, keeping the flat of one hand on the wooden gate, she bent her knees and lowered herself in what is known as The Bunny Dip. She picked up the keys and carefully stood. Then she opened the gate and went along the path to the front door.

I stayed in the shadows for what seemed a very long time waiting for lights to come on in the house. Finally I took a step. I would look through the gate to make sure she'd made it into the house. I would help if necessary. But as I reached the edge of the driveway the lights behind the balcony doors came on. She had not only managed the lock, but had negotiated the stairs to reach the second floor.

I moved along the side of the Volvo until I reached the driver's door and gave it a bump with my hip to close it completely. The dome light went out and I walked back into Mark and David's house.

I tried to go back to sleep, but failed. Giving up, I turned on the lights in the bedroom, dug out the next movie in the chronology and put the cassette in the machine at the foot of the bed.

Joi Lansing's only feature credit in 1960, the year she married Stanley Todd, is *Who Was That Lady?* for Columbia Pictures. While her name is missing from the movie's one-sheet poster, her body is not. Once again Joi's curves are used as a major graphic element to sell a picture. Surrounded by cameo portraits of the film's stars, Tony Curtis (b. 1925), his then wife Janet Leigh, and Dean Martin (1917–1995), is a rendering of Joi in a tight dress leaning down to straighten her stocking. Her face is hidden by a curtain cutting her just above the neck. This pose is lifted from a full-length publicity shot of Joi and co-star Barbara Nichols.

Who Was That Lady?, photographed in black-and-white, is an adaptation of *Who Was That Lady I Saw You With?* a play written by Norman Krasna (1909–1984). It is a libidinous comedy that teaches the lesson that if a man is going to lie to his wife it should be a really big lie.

Opening shots of Columbia University in New York City are accompanied by peppy music composed by André Previn. The sound of a cork popping is followed by animated bubbles dancing at the center of the frame to form the names of the three lead actors.

We arrive at a five-story building on the campus and pick out a man in a white lab coat opening a window on an upper floor. We enter a chemistry lab through the window. The top of the frame is cut off by the bottom of the window, cropping the actors' heads out of the shot. The man in the white coat goes to a lab bench as a young woman enters from frame right, wearing a tight, knee-length dress, her breasts conical to the point of parody. Cool piano noodles on the soundtrack as the headless woman follows the headless man about the room.

The girl's bosom looms into close-up. She approaches the camera and turns. We drop down to fill the screen with her rear. She moves away in pursuit of the man. The camera drops still lower till both actors are cut off at the knees. The man turns to face the woman, stepping into an embrace. The girl raises her left leg to indicated the pleasure of the kiss occurring over our heads.

The office door opens in the background and another woman enters. We push toward her and tilt up to reveal Janet Leigh and her shock at seeing what we do not. On this close-up Dean Martin starts to sing the title song, each word of the first line popping on the screen in time with the music to start the credit sequence.

Janet turns and runs from the lab. Cutting to a reverse from the hall the man in the lab coat is revealed as Tony Curtis, wiping lipstick from his mouth as he comes to the doorway. The girl moves deeper into the background, never showing her face.

Curtis establishes the tone of the movie by reaching up and snatching the accusing question of the title out of the space over his head and throwing the pulsating animated words to the ground before chasing after his wife.

A photo-double for Tony Curtis pursues a photo-double for Janet Leigh across the Columbia campus under the main titles. Promising divorce and ordering Tony to be out of their apartment that night, Janet climbs into a cab in front of a process screen and drives off.

Tony turns for help to his best friend, a womanizing television writer played by Dean Martin. An odd choice for advice on keeping one's marriage intact, but Tony is desperate. Dean comes up with a plan so preposterous it just might work. They will convince Janet that Tony and Dean are both undercover F.B.I. agents and Tony had to kiss that girl as part of a secret mission.

They present this elaborate lie, backed up with a real gun and a fake i.d. Martin has made by the CBS prop department. It's painful watching Janet Leigh struggle to convincingly play someone so naive. She leans into the role with a wide-eyed approach that comes across half gullibility, half Benzedrine. Stretching all credibility, she buys the hoax.

Tony breathes a sigh of relief, but Dean sees infinite opportunities for his pal to enjoy pre-approved infidelity. Any chippy you want becomes a Russian spy and it's your duty to romance her. Which is how Tony and Dean end up on a double date with The Coogle Sisters, Gloria (Barbara Nichols) and Flo (Joi Lansing).

Fifty minutes into the film Dean gets Tony away from Janet by telling her exactly what they're going to do: Meet a couple of girls in booth four at Wong's

Chinese Restaurant on 46th Street near Broadway and try to get them drunk. That part is true, it's the business about the girls being foreign agents and Mr. Wong being with the Taiwan government that shades the facts. But Janet believes it all and kisses her husband before he leaves on this dangerous mission.

Moments later real F.B.I. agent Harry Powell, played by James Whitmore (b. 1921), arrives. Tipped off by the prop man about the gun and fake i.d. he earlier interviewed a gushing Janet. Sensitive to the marital situation he didn't blow the phony setup, a decision he now regrets as he and Janet, with the gun and i.d., head for Wong's Restaurant.

Cut to a high crane shot of a night-for-night backlot New York City street. Dean's white Thunderbird convertible turns the corner and gets a parking space directly in front of Wong's restaurant. The street and sidewalk have been given a wet-down; the pavement is a slick black surface smeared with the reflections of headlights and storefront neon. Shots like this remind you how much better photographed black-and-white movies are compared to color films. All movies suffer on telelvision, but black-and-white has a harder time. At home the small square of gray competes with all the colors in the room. Visually it can't be heard over all the confetti. But in a theater where the image is thirty feet high and the burgundies and golds of the decor are lost in darkness, you're pulled into a carefully lit world, sculpted out of shadows and a spectrum of grays. In black-and-white you see things as they really are.

Tony and Dean enter the restaurant and are shown to their booth, the camera looking back at them as it tracks through the restaurant along a narrow space defined on one side by a row of booths and the other by the bar and a small pocket of a dance floor. Arriving at the booth, Dean orders four Missionary's Downfalls from the bar and Tony sits with his back to the entrance. Tony is worried, Dean confident. Dean looks beyond Tony and tells his friend the girls have arrived. Tony turns.

We look down the length of the restaurant as Joi and Barbara enter wearing identical shimmering halter dresses gathered at the hip like sarongs. They carry identical plastic handbags that look like small tool boxes. The two women hit their marks and stand side by side at the converging parallel elements of the composition, Joi to the left of Barbara. There is a vertiginous zoom worthy of a Tex Avery cartoon that moves in on their bodies, cropping off their heads. This movie is fixated on decapitating voluptuous women.

While brass vibrates on the soundtrack, Joi leans forward to bring her cleavage into the tighter shot, reaching down and running her hands along her leg to smooth a stocking. Barbara touches Joi's ear, adjusting her earring and they push off, walking toward us along the length of the restaurant. We track ahead of them as they come. It's a remarkable shot.

Cinematographer Harry Straddling, Sr. (1901–1970), who photographed Joi at M.G.M. in the 1948 Arthur Freed production *Easter Parade*, puts his camera at waist height, looking slightly up at them, holding the low ceiling with its overhead fans constantly slicing the actors with blades of shadow. The narrow space becomes a runway for The Coogle Sisters, a presentational space with which they appear familiar.

Did women ever really look like this?

No offense to Miss Nichols, but Joi is astonishing. She's thirty-two years old here and that ripeness adds something to her body and face. Her platinum hair was made for black-and-white film and her brief screen time in this minor movie is some of her most striking. Observe the smile on her face. That "Yes, I really do look this good" expression as men turn in their wake.

The restaurant is a dark place and you suddenly realize what's been bothering you about the look of the picture. This comedy doesn't have the sort of high-key lighting usually associated with farce. Straddling, who photographed three movies for Alfred Hitchcock, has lit the scene and the picture as if it were a gritty crime movie.

The women reach the booth and settle in between the two men, Joi next to Dean who claims her as his date and Barbara next to Tony. Introductions over, Barbara reaches for a plate of appetizer cookies, picks one then puts it down.

"I have to be careful what I swallow today," she explains.

A look from Tony to Dean and a close-up of a smirking Dean load the line with an amazing amount of fallatial overtones.

"I was poisoned last night," she tells the men. "I ate some lousy swordfish. It's stuck right here."

She points to her cleavage.

Martin comments, "That fish knows what it's doing."

All that's missing are the rim shots.

The Coogle Sisters are performers recently turned down for Ted Mack's Amateur Hour.

"Mr. Mack said he wouldn't put us on," Joi tells the boys.

Barbara explains, "He said we didn't look like amateurs."

Ba-doom-boom.

Dean proceeds to compound all previous lies by telling the girls Tony is a vice president at CBS.

Joi lights up. "We're very versatile. We sing and dance."

"Like rabbits," Dean says.

The drinks arrive, tall exotic glasses surmounted by paper fans.

Joi offers a toast: "Well, here's looking through you!"

We cut to the entrance of the restaurant as Janet and F.B.I. agent Whitmore enter from the street and are shown to a booth from which they can observe the men and their dates. I was all of ten when I saw this movie at The Cascade so many of the single-minded double-entendres sailed clear over my head. But I remember there was a Huckleberry Hound cartoon playing on the television over the bar. Movies change so much with puberty.

When Joi and Barbara head for the ladies room Janet takes the opportunity to sneak over to the table and reassure Tony and Dean that she's there with F.B.I. back-up. She then tails The Coogle Sisters into the powder room. Tony and Dean see the real F.B.I. agent sitting in the other booth, smiling at them like Madame Lafarge.

The ladies room of Wong's Restaurant looks like a clip-joint in prewar Singapore. We discover Barbara on the pay phone calling their agent, Joi at her shoulder, waiting through yet another phone call. Janet enters and overhears one side of the conversation. The agent wises the girls to the fact that Dean is handing them a line. Hanging up Gloria tells her sister they should just get rid of the men. Janet is certain this means the two women are planning to assassinate Tony and Dean.

Janet gets out of the ladies room first and returns to Whitmore terrified that her husband is about to be murdered by foreign agents. Whitmore, knowing the truth, is unconcerned. He goes to call his office from a phone booth next to the bar and put an end to this bothersome impersonation. This is a movie from a time when we were not in continuous conversation with each other. If you wanted to call someone on the telephone you had to go someplace where you could find a phone and hope the person you wanted to speak to was at the location you were calling.

The Coogle Sisters return to the booth armed with the information that Dean's offer of a weekend in Atlantic City won't help their careers any more than it will their reputations. They start to give the boys a hard time, but Tony and Dean hustle them out of the restaurant hoping to avoid their fate. Janet sees them leave and, fearing for her husband's life, goes after them with the gun Tony left behind.

Tony and Dean are trying to get the Coogles into the Thunderbird when Janet bursts out of the restaurant, gun drawn. The intent look on Janet's face as she pushes through the crowd of extras on the sidewalk, the deep focus as she extends her arm with the revolver, the gun looming like a cannon on the left side of the frame, remind you again this is not how comedy is normally photographed.

Panic on the sidewalk. The Coogles scream, the men flinch. Whitmore catches up with Janet and tries to wrestle the gun from her. She holds it over her head as hands reach up to grab it. The gun fires and Whitmore is shot in the arm.

We cut to a high shot of the wet street and the restaurant as the crowd congeals around the entrance. It looks like a shot from another movie Harry Straddling photographed: *A Face in the Crowd.*

While the wounded Whitmore goes back into the restaurant followed by Dean Martin, Janet Leigh confronts The Coogle Sisters. This puts her face to face with Joi, closer than the two actresses were three years earlier when Janet stood next to Joi, seated in another white convertible, at the border checkpoint in *Touch of Evil.*

Did Janet remember Joi? Or did she have no memory of the blonde she never really looked at in the moments before she exploded?

A face familiar to those who grew up watching The Three Stooges shorts appears at an open window above the restaurant. Emil Sitka (1914–1998) leans out to see what's happening and dislodges a potted plant that slides down the awning and crashes on Tony Curtis' head rendering him unconscious.

Sitka, the oldest of five children raised with his brothers and sisters in a Catholic convent in Pittsburgh, Pennsylvania, was under contract to Columbia Pictures for more than two decades. He appeared in thirty-five Stooges shorts, usually playing a scatterbrained scientist or a butler or a lunatic in films such as *Space Ship Sappy, Jerks of All Trades,* and *Pardon My Wrench.* In *Brideless Groom* he's the Justice of the Peace trying to complete a marriage ceremony in the face of mounting slapstick violence, repeating his mantra, "Hold hands, you love birds."

Janet goes to her comatose husband. We drop back for another high angle on the street scene, watching the action through a trapezoidal window frame in a building across the street. At this angle it looks like the building is canted out over the street a good thirty degrees like something from *The Last Laugh.*

The press arrives as Janet cradles Tony in her arms. A CBS camera truck pulls up to the curb. This is a version of New York City where the firing of a single shot near Times Square is big news. A television camera with two large floodlights is pushed into a shot that puts the two glowing globes adjacent to Joi's breasts as she stands on the sidewalk.

Tony regains consciousness, sees the t.v. camera, hears his wife describing him to the live audience as an F.B.I. agent and faints dead away. Fade to black. The Coogle Sisters are referred to briefly in the next scene, but never seen again.

In the aftermath of their evening with The Coogles, Tony and Dean are kidnapped by real foreign agents led by Belka, played by Simon Oakland (1915–1983) who earlier that year appeared in the coda to *Psycho* (Paramount, 1960) as Dr. Richmond, the psychiatrist who explains the mental motivations behind Janet Leigh's murder.

Drugged and confused, Tony and Dean wake in the boiler room of The Empire State Building. Looking at their surroundings they conclude they're aboard a Russian submarine and decide to destroy the sub as an act of patriotism. What they do by turning every wheel and tripping every lever they can find is disrupt the skyscraper's heating and cooling systems. The last shot of the movie depicts a mushroom cloud of smoke and steam rising from the observation deck of the landmark building and spreading out over Manhattan. It's not the first time the skyline looked like that.

On the morning of July 28, 1945, Lt. Colonel William Franklin Smith, Jr. was ferrying the B-25D Billy Mitchell class bomber "Old John Feather Merchant" from Bedford Army Air Field in Massachusetts to Newark Field in New Jersey when he made a fatal mistake in the fog choked skies above New York City. Mistaking Roosevelt Island for the much larger Manhattan Island, Lt. Colonel Smith turned prematurely and within moments had banked over the RCA Building at 53rd Street and was flying south along Fifth Avenue at an altitude of approximately one thousand feet. At 9:55 A.M. the three-engine bomber, traveling two hundred miles an hour, struck the north face of The Empire State Building at the level of the 79th Floor where The Catholic War Relief Services had their offices.

One engine and part of the landing gear traveled through the building coming out the south side and fell to the roof of The Waldorff Building, while the bulk of the burning wreckage rained down on 34th Street. Eleven people were killed in the building and the crew of three died on the aircraft.

That morning my mother was at her job as a teller at The Chase Manhattan Bank branch office located in the lobby of The Empire State Building. She felt the impact shudder through the building and at first thought it was a Japanese suicide attack. The bank employees were evacuated from the building to a bar across the street. She remembered stepping over smoking debris in the middle of 34th Street.

By the time she walked to Pennslvania Station that evening for the ride back to Long Island the story was front page news. Sitting in the coach as it rattled under the East River, she pointed to the picture on the front of the Daily News, smoke and flames pouring out of the 79th floor and disappearing into the fog that still obscured the top of the building.

"I was there," she said.

The man holding the paper looked at her.

"What?"

"I said, I was there."

Within seconds the news spread the length of the railway car.

"This girl says she was there."

"What happened?"

My mother told them about being at her cage, about the muffled thud they all felt, about the scraping shriek of the elevator dropping eighty floors through the shaft on the other side of the wall at her back. About how the firemen came to get them out and walked them across the street, about the smell of burning gasoline and hot metal.

She was the most interesting person on that train and the people listened to her, hanging on her every word, all the way home. No one had ever paid that much attention to her. Not her family, not even her husband.

When the train pulled in at her station, did she think about staying on, riding to the end of the line, making the moment and the sense that she mattered last as long as she could?

She didn't though. She got off the train and everything went back to normal.

Joi would continue to find work in television, but it would be five years before she appeared in another feature film, and that next role would be her last in a major studio movie.

Gray light outside the window. I should try to get some sleep.

I closed the blinds and the drapes then crawled back into bed and buried my face in the pillows to hide from the light. I slept some, but not much and by 8:30 I was in my car driving to the harbor shops in search of a Sunday Times.

The clouds were low and thick, less dry brush watercolor, more tempera.

The early drive for the Sunday papers plus the twinges of sympathetic hangover I felt when I thought about my neighbor reminded me of my first months in Los Angeles. Saturday nights spent in the solitary consumption of sweet wine followed by Sundays filled with coffee, Excedrin and the pledge to seek human company before a habit turned into a problem.

The shops at the harbor are supposed to feel like a village surrounding the clustered verticals of ships' masts. The tenants don't work very hard at this illusion and I think everybody's grateful for that. No place there sold newspapers, but I was able to get a cardboard cup of coffee that tasted like burnt popcorn.

I walked along the edge of the marina, past one of the restaurants in the harbor village that faced the water with three large windows. The center pane was missing and two men with beards and ponytails were positioning a sheet of plywood to cover the hole. I crunched through a gravel of blue-green safety glass sprayed across the pavement. The window had been broken out, not in.

When I'd had all of the coffee I could stand, I tossed the dregs and walked to my car, then past it, out of the parking lot and across the access road to reach the scrub covered dunes facing the ocean. Gray sky, green choppy water and to my right a low spine of crushed rock the color of hematite reaching out a few hundred yards to shelter the harbor entrance. There were darker, more burdensome clouds to the north, over Ventura and the road to Santa Paula.

A patch of sky opened over the sea, maybe a mile beyond the breakers. Light shafted down and for a moment the whitecaps burned like magnesium. Then the clouds closed again and the beam of light was gone.

I wonder if my neighbor was in that restaurant last night. The one with the broken window.

Joi Lansing's final appearance in a major studio release was in *Marriage on the Rocks* from Warner Bros. in 1965. The only remarkable thing about this movie, a leaden farce about a marital mix-up between ad agency partners Frank Sinatra and Dean Martin, is how Joi's brief appearance in the movie generated so much publicity material.

In addition to stills shot on the set during production there are portrait shots of her in each of her costume changes. There are so many pictures of Joi in one blue and white polka-dot bikini she must have spent more time at the publicity shoots than in front of the movie cameras. She's pictured in the swim suit standing over a vintage typewriter, on the telephone, adjusting the suit's straps while looking through the camera at us, a small "ooh" forming on her lips. This last image appeared on the film's posters and on giant cutouts of Joi mounted to theater marquees during the movie's initial release.

Marriage on the Rocks tells the story of how, for reasons we don't need to explore, Dean Martin and Frank Sinatra both end up married to Deborah Kerr (b. 1921). Sequentially, not simultaneously. Joi plays Lola, secretary to and presumably lover of the man she drank Missionary's Downfalls with in *Who Was That Lady?*, bachelor Dean Martin. She shows up in five scenes, one without dialogue, for less than five minutes of screen time, vanishing from the picture long before it grinds to a halt.

Joi is first sighted shortly after the main titles in the ad agency offices where she brings a message to Dean Martin. Half an hour of laborious whimsy oozes across the screen before we see Joi again. And there it is, the famous polka-dot bikini that shows up in countless stills and key art. The scene, consisting of a single wide two-shot of Joi and Dean, lasts less than two minutes.

Joi soothes her boss on the deck at Dean's beach house, one of those sprawling places that exist only in American movies, where people come home to the circular fireplace already lit and the wraparound windows afford a panoramic view of a smogless backdrop hung from the rigging of a soundstage. Martin is on a high-backed chaise, Joi leans over him administering a back rub. She's all breasts and platinum hair, her lower body cut off by the back of the chaise. Joi suggests Dean communicate with partner Frank who is in Mexico to divorce wife Deborah Kerr. Perhaps a letter.

The camera dollies right as Dean gets off the chaise and moves to a type-writer on a patio table. The rest of Joi is revealed when she steps out from behind the chaise. The bottom of her bathing suit is cut low across her hips with a short dust-ruffle of a skirt. When she turns we get a glimpse of how the top of her costume was constructed to present her augmented breasts as dra-matically as possible. It's more of a sling than a bra and it seems doubtful someone could get into it without assistance.

This is the most flesh Joi Lansing ever showed in a movie. Her healthy diet and exercises resulted in a body that's trim, but not skinny. Her ribs are visible from the side, but there's muscle anywhere you choose to look. She's impres-sive enough on television, but on a movie screen the impact of that figure pho-tographed once again by William Daniels in Technicolor and Panavision must have been breathtaking.

She would have worn a robe from her dressing room to the stage, her body thick with make-up from head to toe to keep her from washing out under the lights. The feature stages at Warner Bros. are Brobdingnagian boxes with inte-rior heights of eighty feet or more, the insides of their curved roofs hidden by a crosshatching of catwalks and lighting grids. You have to cross much confusion and darkness to get from the door of a soundstage to a set, threading your way through fifty or more people, mostly men, and their equipment to find the island of intense light in front of the camera. Stepping into that light she slipped off the robe. A wardrobe person took it lightly from her shoulders and the set make-up woman examined Joi's body for smudges and creases.

I imagine a falling away of sound, a quieting of voices and a stuttering end to the work as the crew realized she was there. She had been walking onto sets big and small for almost twenty years at that point, listening for the impact she had on the men around her, consciously or unconsciously taking inventory of the effect, using the hush to measure her success.

Joi and Dean move to the table, but it's Dean Martin who sits down at the portable typewriter. Joi hovers over him as he starts pecking out a letter. She's his secretary, but he has to do the typing. It's a joke.

End of scene. End of bikini. But the memory lingers.

Things happen to the leads then Joi shows up in a leopard skin coat with matching hat to tell Dean she has to visit a sick relative. She leaves him with a replacement secretary who will be safe from his advances because she's married.

Still later Joi returns to eat dinner with Dean by his fireplace. She is without real function in the scene. The shot of Dean trying to get Frank on the phone in Mexico is over Joi, her hair and a slice of lime green sweater visible on the left side of the wide screen. This is how she spent much of her time in features: As the back of a head at the edge of a shot of the movie's star.

Joi's final scene in the movie occurs after a series of implausible plot twists leave Dean with Frank's wife and family and Frank with Dean's swinging bachelor lifestyle, including secretary Lola. Dean and Frank are in what used to be Frank's office with the woman who used to be his secretary, Miss Blight, played by the stalwart Kathleen Freeman (1919–2001) who made a fifty year career out of playing secretaries, P.T.A. members, club ladies and assorted busybodies. She is also the scarf enveloped speech teacher Phoebe Dinsmore in *Singin' in the Rain*.

With Frank, Dean and Kathleen in the foreground Joi enters through a door upstage center wearing the most impressive dress of her career.

Costumes are built, not sewn and the construction concept is particularly appropriate in talking about this formfitting halter dress designed to support and showcase every curve and contour of Joi Lansing's body. The dress was built by Walter Plunkett (1902–1982) who began work in silent films, moved up the ranks at RKO, worked on *Gone With the Wind*, and went to Metro-Goldwyn-Mayer in the late 1940s. At M.G.M. he worked on several films produced by Arthur Freed including *Singin' in the Rain*. While he designed Kathleen Freeman's wardrobe, Joi, as an extra, was probably put in an existing costume. Walter Plunkett also designed the men's wardrobe for *Forbidden Planet* (M.G.M., 1954), costumes that would later be rented to the producers of *Queen of Outer Space* which is how Joi ended up hugging a Plunkett uniform during her brief appearance in that film.

Paler than Joi's eyes, the faintly green halter slings around her neck and strains at the job of containing her. This sense of barely controlled flesh is heightened by the three small buttons below her cleavage, visibly stressed by their task. Tightly belted, the skirt cutting her at the knee, she's more fully clothed than in her bikini, but this dress is more overtly about sexual presentation than her other changes.

She steps into the office to call Mr. Sinatra away. Sinatra exits the office, taking us to a shot of Joi, cutting her below the hip in a composition usually referred to as a "cowboy" since it would allow us to see her guns if she were wearing any.

Joi stands there after Sinatra exits, winking at us and her old boss during a music cue unctuous with saxophones. A beat and Sinatra returns, taking Joi by the upper arm. A look to Dean and to us communicating "Sorry, old pal, this is mine now," and he whisks her out of the office.

The last we see of Joi is her blonde hair and bare back. In this fashion Joi exits the office, the movie, and her career in mainstream feature films.

Aside from its complete failure as entertainment *Marriage on the Rocks* reopens the Frank Sinatra issue.

Joi is mentioned twice in *His Way*, Kitty Kelley's voluminous and unauthorized biography of Frank Sinatra. Sinatra's long time make-up man Beans Ponedel lumps Joi Lansing with Natalie Wood and Shirley MacLaine among others, saying how "He was real good to his girls. He gave them all parts in his movies."

Jacqueline Park, who Kelly identifies as "an actress who later became the mistress of Jack Warner," is quoted on several topics including Sinatra's relationship with Lansing: "When Joi Lansing, who was a regular bedmate of Frank's for years, was dying of leukemia, he paid for all her hospital bills."

Joi died of breast cancer aggravated by anemia, not leukemia, but that's a credible mistake. It's the awkwardness of the quote that trips me. I mean, aside from Walter Winchell, who drops phrases like "regular bedmate" into their conversation?

Would it be possible for someone like Joi Lansing to work with Frank Sinatra and not be one of the rapacious singer's conquests? Perhaps once. But Lansing worked on several Sinatra productions between 1958 and 1965.

You want her to be the one who didn't submit to the bully because she's the one you like. You get the same burn of impotent frustration you felt seeing the girl you had the crush on clinging to the popular quarterback on the way to homeroom. She looks up at him in acknowledgment of what he's doing for her status or, worse, true admiration. He keeps his hand casually around her waist as he looks ahead with a practiced half smile, unaware that he is peaking way too early and all those varsity awards and newspaper clippings will end up tarnishing and turning yellow in his cubicle at the Chevrolet dealership.

One t.v. special, she could have ducked him. The first movie, perhaps. But the second movie, with a Dean Martin picture in-between? Not that it makes any difference now. I just don't like to be reminded how High School never ends.

While Joi Lansing would never again appear in a movie produced by a major studio the same can not be said for her wardrobe.

In 1967 Warner Bros. produced *Hotel* based on an Arthur Hailey novel about the intersecting lives of the staff and guests of a venerable New Orleans Hotel. Edith Head received credit for the gowns and Howard Shoup for the rest of the wardrobe, but neither designed the costume worn by an uncredited day-player appearing as a prostitute in a French Quarter strip club.

Soon after the initial round of exposition to set up the films multiple plot lines, we cut into a seedy club where a blonde woman is sweet talking a conventioneer out of his room key with the promise that she will be in the room when he returns to the hotel later. He agrees, gives her the key, then shifts his bulk out of the booth and departs.

The girl slides the key into her décolletage, its plastic fob hanging at her heart like a broach. She unfolds herself from the booth and crosses the floor to the bar built in front of the strippers' stage. It's on the cross when we see her full-figure that we recognize the outfit. It is the same faintly green halter dress Joi Lansing wore in her final scene two years earlier.

The actress in *Hotel* fills out the dress to the best of her ability, playing with the key fob that covers the three buttons Plunkett added to re-enforce Joi's pneumatic qualities. Reaching the bar she sits next to professional hotel thief Karl Malden (b. 1912) and opens negotiations for the sale of the key. In the background between them a stripper dances. The stripper is not an important part of the scene and does not reappear in the movie, but she will wind up on the movie's one-sheet poster and other advertising art, a marginal figure moved to the footlights like a dancing girl brought out to sucker men into a midway show, or Joi Lansing on any of a hundred posters and lobby cards.

Gloria, the newswoman who briefly shared a closet with me at the radio station, eventually gave up her Rhineskeller ways and married Rick, one of the airtime salesmen. The station manager, who some of us suspected of having slept with Gloria, arranged Rick's bachelor party at a windowless bunker of a bar outside Pittsburgh. The bar featured what was called at the time "Topless Entertainment." Later these places evolved into Gentlemen's Clubs which are to Burlesque what McDonald's is to restaurants.

The place of Rick the Salesman's bachelor party was filled with refrigerated air burdened with a decade of recycled cigarette smoke. There was a bar, some tables and a long, narrow stage with reflective contact paper along the edge. Music came from a pair of washing machine-sized black speakers at either side of the stage.

When we arrived there was a girl on stage dressed in jeans and flannel shirt. Her hair was in a dirty blonde ponytail, the shirt open. She wore no bra or make-up and moved unenthusiastically from side to side, indifferent to the beat as The Rolling Stones lamented their lack of satisfaction.

There were ten of us which tripled the size of the audience. We split between two tables uncomfortably close to the stage and yelled our drink orders to a waitress in her late forties who never looked at us. The drinks came, mine in a glass with a greasy thumbprint on the side.

The Rolling Stones stopped and so did the girl on stage. Her finale consisted of walking across the stage, picking up her shirt and leaving.

Bachman Turner Overdrive shook the big speakers and another girl came on stage with the same dead-eyed look as her predecessor. She was in jeans and a t-shirt and I started to suspect the place recruited their entire program from the runaway girls loitering around the Port Authority Bus Terminal.

As this second girl rapidly removed her shirt to expose her breasts the waitress returned. This time she looked at us, but we didn't know why. She stood there for a few seconds then walked away, returning with the bouncer we'd passed on the way into the bar. He stood between us and the stage and had no trouble being heard over the music.

"One drink minimum."

We looked at him. One of us held up his beer to indicate we had complied with the stated policy. The bouncer, who had no neck, his head growing directly out of his shoulders like a stalk of asparagus, told us:

"One drink minimum for each girl."

We were expected to buy a fresh round every time a different performer took the stage. There was no room for negotiation so another watery rum and Coke arrived in another glass, this one with something white and crusty on the rim.

I left both my drinks on the table and got up before the second dancer completed her routine of strolling back and forth on stage. I walked past the bouncer and out to the parking lot.

The club was in what was euphemistically called a transitional neighborhood. Once probably farm land, it had been converted to light industry after the war. When the economy collapsed places like the club I'd just escaped moved in.

Across the four-lane county road was another failing enterprise: The Twin-Hi-Way Drive-in Movie Theater. The marquee promised they were merely closed for the season, but the weeds in the wide driveway told a less optimistic story.

They will tell you the reasons behind the demise of the drive-in movie are shifting demographics, growing audience sophistication and the need to squeeze the most money out of the real estate. This may be true, but it isn't the reason. The drive-in movie has been condemned in order to blind people to the real crime: Today's mainstream movie is a bloodless, hothouse creation that can't survive in the outside world. Inbred and over-marketed, as fragile as an orchid, it would evaporate during a three hundred foot throw through a cool summer night and vanish before reaching the monumental screen.

Behind me I heard the end of *Taking Care of Business*. Rod Stewart started to sing. Somewhere in that grim box the man who would marry Gloria ordered another drink and another disinterested girl came to the stage.

I walked to the edge of the parking lot and looked across to the Drive-in. Ten years earlier the stripper from *Hotel* might have glistened across the concrete screen of The Twin-Hi-Way, a dancing giant under a summer moon. A phantom made out of colored light, yet so much more arrousing and memorable than the reality behind me.

Malden and the young woman reach an understanding. She lifts the key from her bosom and exchanges it for cash. The actress wearing Joi's costume exits frame left and does not reappear in the picture. The dress was cleaned, catalogued and packed away.

The likelihood of this outfit still existing in any recognizable form is remote. A few years after the Plunkett costume was stored a second time the major studios went through a frantic disgorging of props, costumes and real estate, selling off their history in an effort to survive financial mismanagement.

There would have been no reason to consider the costume worthy of preservation.

I needed to clear my head before plunging into the final years of Joi's career so I put on my coat and left Mark and David's house. I thought I'd walk along the beach, but as I started that way I saw my neighbor headed in the same direction. She was wearing sweats and a knit cap and was talking on her cell phone, apparently no worse for wear after last night.

I turned and went the other way, to the end of the street, through the back parking lot of MILK-LIQUOR-LOTTO, then across Harbor Boulevard. I crossed a canal and walked along the edge of Mandalay Villas, "A Master-planned Community" of townhouses, hundreds of them, in different phases of construction, spreading across the horizon like PictSweet mushrooms.

California is being consumed by homes. Hillsides and salt marshes are being turned into faux towns patterned after the backlot suburbia behind the soundstages at Universal. But that mock town had more diversity than these developments where the houses swell with square-footage, but have no back-yards and the windows afford a beautiful view of your neighbor's windows.

The new houses line new streets named Wave Crest and Outrigger near the water and Canyon and Sage in the hills. Streets named by developers who remember how Levittown imposed the status of community on arbitrary sections by naming all the streets in one grid after flowers, another zone after birds, or Poet's Corner with Blake and Whittier, Dickinson and Shelley.

I wanted to see how big Mandalay Villas was, but the end of it was still ahead of me when the sky darkened, touched the roofs of the unfinished town-houses and it started to drizzle. I turned back, pulling up the hood of my coat. I'm not looking forward to what's waiting for me back at Mark and David's house.

I approach Joi's last films with growing dread. I know what she's in for and realize my mistake. I should never have put these things in order. I should have left them unconnected, uncorrelated. Encountered randomly, her movies are one thing, but put them in sequence and the arc of the career is clear. Only it's not an arc, more of a plateau. Something lower. A butte, with a steep drop at the edge.

Hot Cars and *The Atomic Submarine* were not towering accomplishments, but they have a level of craftsmanship missing from the final films. They had, if not pride, at least the desire to actively avoid shame; an impulse absent from the two movies I'm about to describe to you.

They are insignificant pictures. Their failure doesn't matter. But they were the last things she did, and last things should be important. They should have some feeling of summation. The only thing Joi Lansing's last movies summarize is the yawning distance between M.G.M. in 1948 and the cramped confines of Colorvision Studios where interiors for *Big Foot* were shot at the end of the sixties.

The unavoidable truth is this: When Joi was at the edge of the frame, the pictures were better. The closer she got to the center ring, the worse the movies became. This was never her fault. Joi remains the same; committed, enthusiastic, full of energy, but the projects become less and less thought-out, more shoddy. Her only sin was being a dependable fall-back choice. Joi never got a role until a half-dozen others turned it down. Christ, Mamie Van Doren walked away from *Hillbillys in a Haunted House*. The exception, perhaps, is *Touch of Evil*.

I think Welles was being very specific when he picked her for that near faceless role, this woman he once described as "standing for something greater than talent, greater than beauty." It may have been a private joke between Welles and Joi, but it was a deliberate joke.

Welles is gone and so are all the other people who had lives before they started making movies, the ones who understood what movies meant to people, how they changed the way we saw ourselves and the world, taught us how to light a cigarette, what love was supposed to feel like, how to face death. Now the responsibility for teaching those lessons rests with the people who came up with Aunt Jamima and The Campbell Soup Kids. Powerful tools for communication have been placed in the hands of people with absolutely nothing to say.

Boredom was once the gatekeeper of creativity. It was the force that disqualified the amateur and turned away the dilettantes. But the machines have overthrown boredom and we're suffering the consequences. We've created a technology that's powerful and indulgent. It removes effort and that is the fatal flaw, because making an effort, the fact that a task is difficult, that it requires inspiration, skill and possibly talent, is what makes it worth doing. Today the undemocratic distribution of talent has become irrelevant. A hundred years of subtle filmmaking grammar has been reduced to point-and-click software. Anyone can make a movie. The result is a drawer full of glass doorknobs.

It was raining by the time I reached MILK-LIQUOR-LOTTO, the sky a rolling lead. It was going to be a prolonged and soaking rain.

We come now to the final two features in the canon, productions so threadbare they qualify as motion pictures on technical terms only.

Produced in 1967 by The Woolner Brothers, *Hillbillys in a Haunted House* is a sequel to the previous year's *Las Vegas Hillbillys*. I point out the indefinite article in the title: A Haunted House instead of the more specific The Haunted House, suggesting the generalized approach adopted by the production itself.

Ferlin Husky (b. 1925) returns as country western singer Woody along with his sidekick, the allegedly humorous Jeepers played by Don Bowman (b. 1937). Joi appears as Woody's traveling companion and assumed love interest Boots Malone, a role created in the first film by Mamie Van Doren (b. 1933).

Directed by Jean Yarbrough (1900–1975), a journeyman director with credits dating back to the 1920s including several Abbott and Costello features and *Hot Shots* (Allied Artists, 1956) featuring Joi Lansing and the aging survivors of The Bowery Boys, and written by Duke Yelton who appears to have no other credits of any kind, *Hillbillys in a Haunted House* is little more than a series of country western acts strung together with a randomness matched only by its lack of invention. It's so close to not being a movie at all, you wonder what force of nature is holding the image to the surface of the film.

The story concerns three singers, Woody, Boots and Jeepers making their way to a big Jamboree in Nashville. They are waylaid and forced to spend a night in an abandoned house thought to be haunted, but is in truth the headquarters of foreign agents bent on stealing a rocket fuel formula from a nearby missile base. The trio thwart the spies and continue on to the big show in Nashville.

Synopsis such as this often do a disservice to the film they describe. Such is not the case here. If anything I have overstated the dramatic coherency and entertainment value of *Hillbillys in a Haunted House*.

Following the credits which are superimposed over a bluish day-for-night shot of a large house that doesn't look haunted so much as foreclosed, a wide, white Pontiac convertible approaches us along a country road. The car has a set of steer horns for a hood ornament and is otherwise festooned with horseshoes, rifles and six-gun door handles. Sanitized country music twangs on the soundtrack as we cut to the same car in front of a process screen. Ferlin Husky as Woody is at the wheel. In the front passenger seat is Joi in a shinny turquoise blouse. Visible between them in the back seat is Jeepers.

They sing to an overly reverbed playback of how they are "Going to Nashville for a Swinging Jamboree." At least Woody and Boots sing of their excitement. Jeepers' lyrics are about how he suffers from car sickness. Husky and Bowman essentially jog through the movie, neither making an effort to bring even a passing interest to the project. In this opening scene Husky appears embarrassed by the need to pretend to be driving the big car. He's also less than enthusiastic about matching his performance on the playback.

Joi is, of course, totally committed to the song, the theatricality of the process shot and the entire enterprise. After all, this film will give her more contiguous screen time than any picture has in more than a decade.

The song over, the happy trio finds itself driving into a pitched gun battle between government agents and spies who swarm around nearby Acme City Missile Base. After the skirmish, Boots convinces Woody that Jeepers needs a rest before they continue on to Nashville. They pull into a gas station where the attendant tells them that while Acme City is teaming with espionage and government contracts it lacks accommodations. There's no hotel, but perhaps the three might stay at the old Beauregard mansion. It's been abandoned for years, but at least they'll stay dry, ducking the stock footage thunderstorm gathering above them. Only after Boots, Woody and Jeepers have driven off does the station attendant realize he's omitted an important piece of information.

"Wait," he yells at the retreating Pontiac, then, to himself as well as the audience, "I forgot to tell them it's haunted."

The Pontiac reaches the old Beauregard place. Once out of the car and in the cheap haunted house set we get a good look at Joi's wardrobe. She glows in tight white pants and boots, a thin yellow scarf for a belt, and that turquoise blouse.

Woody sings to calm Jeepers. Then another group of musicians shows up. "We thought this place was empty." They perform two numbers before being frightened away by a skeleton hanging inside a picture frame over the mantel. Joi's reaction shots are cut into these musical numbers with no particular rhythm or purpose. It reminds me how much of her career was spent looking entertained, interested, aroused, afraid, or whatever was required.

What would it look like if you stitched together all those singles and close-ups from all those movies, assembling a string of reactions taking you through hair styles, film stocks and make-up adjustments? The expressions would be the same, but you could watch her go from her twenties to her forties like a time-lapse nature film of an exotic flower.

With the under-cranked departure of the other band we cut to a dungeon somewhere. We assume it's in the house, but it could be anywhere. We have arrived in this space of flats painted with stones and a collection of vaguely scientific panels and lights without benefit of any transition that might tell us where we are. It must be the house. Why else would the filmmakers be showing it to us?

In the dungeon we meet a gang of spies including Basil Rathbone (1892–1967), John Carradine (1906–1988) and Lon Chaney, Jr. (1906–1973), three actors of advanced age whose careers are beyond the power of this film to tarnish. There is also a gorilla named Anatole played by George Barrows (1914–1994) who in 1953 wore an antenna-sprouting space helmet atop his ape suit to play Ro-Man in the infamous *Robot Monster*. They are led by a sinister Dragon Lady character named Madame Wong played by Linda Ho, an Asian actress with a thick accent who has substantial difficulty navigating her way around the oft repeated name "Beauregard."

After repeated viewings it becomes clear whole sections of the movie have been shoved together out of order in an effort to accelerate the plot. This results in characters referring back to scenes that haven't happened yet. Eventually we glean the spies are waiting for instructions from Dr. Fu before proceeding with the theft of the rocket formula. The spies discuss how nothing must be done till the instructions come then proceed not to do it.

Upstairs, Boots, Woody and Jeepers explore the house, reaching a bedroom suite that is clean of fake cobwebs. Joi opens a closet filled with dresses and wonders if this was the room of a southern belle back in plantation days.

There is a ripply dissolve to Joi alone in the room wearing a long, white satin gown. There's a large bow in her hair, a satin sash around her waist tied in a bow at the back and two satin roses at her décolletage, all the same color as the blouse she wears in the rest of the movie. I'm stunned someone on this thoroughly throwaway production would bother to get such a small detail right. Did anyone notice?

Joi sings the song *Gowns*, one of her two solo numbers in the picture. She sings to herself in the mirror while holding other gowns, spraying herself with perfume, turning herself admiringly, filling the orchestral bridge with anything she can think of.

It's impossible to keep your mind from wandering while trying to watch this movie. One of the places I go is to wonder what posterity would think, what could it possibly conclude, if *Hillbillys in a Haunted House* was the only movie to survive some species extinguishing event. Imagine this was the only picture left to speak to the future of who we were.

We return to the dungeon where nothing continues to happen. At one point Rathbone and Carradine talk about where they should vacation after the mission is complete. Or are the actors planning their escape from the movie itself? Meanwhile, Lon Chaney, Jr. is again called on to parody his own performance in the 1940 film of John Steinbeck's *Of Mice and Men*. Here Anatole the gorilla is substituted for Lenny's rabbits.

Upstairs with Boots and the boys, songs are shoehorned into the movie like sex scenes in a porno, stopping what little story momentum there is dead in its tracks.

Jeepers sits down to watch the television they brought in from the car, the set being something they apparently travel with. Merle Haggard appears on the television screen and starts to sing. Jeepers watches him and we watch Jeepers watch. Rathbone and Carradine inexplicably appear on the television screen staring out at Jeepers while Haggard sings such lyrics as "Hi there, shoes. Are you the ones she wore last night?"

Later Anatole the gorilla is sent to grab Boots and bring her to the dungeon for some unexplained reason. The gorilla snatches Joi behind the backs of Woody and Jeepers standing less than three feet away. Only the intervention of the film editor prevents us from seeing the abduction in one crowded shot.

Boots is taken to the dungeon and tied to a chair. As the villains debate if they should question Boots or wait ("Let's wait." "Are you sure?" "We can start to question her.") one suspects Joi and the handful of remaining audience members have stumbled into a Monogram Pictures interpretation of *Waiting for Godot* with Basil Rathbone and John Carradine as Vladimir and Estrogon. Lon Chaney, Jr. must be Pozzo which would make the gorilla Lucky. But what about Madame Wong who, having battled the word "Beauregard," is now confronted with dialogue containing "Alamogordo"?

The interrogation begins with Joi telling the villains her name is Boots Malone. Carradine and Rathbone analyze the name for hidden meaning, breaking it down into syllables and volleying the sounds back and forth.

"Malone. Malone. Ma-lone. Ma. Lone. Ma. Ma. Ma."

"Is it Pozzo or Bozzo?"

Deciding long after we have that this line of inquiry is going nowhere, Didi and Gogo order Lon to transfer Boots to a spikeless iron maiden sitting among the scientific flotsam and jetsam. Joi is pushed into the iron maiden and Chaney starts to close the doors. But the maiden can't contain Joi's bounty, the doors pinch at the blue fabric of the blouse and she has to skootch out of the way so they can close.

This is followed by another action packed scene with Rathbone and Carradine discussing how long it will take them to move all their spy equipment.

"Let's start dismantling it now."

"No, we better wait till we hear from Dr. Fu."

"We should have heard from him by now."

"Well? Shall we go?"

"Yes, let's go."

They do not move.

Samuel Barclay Beckett (1906–1989) was in New York City during the summer of 1964 working with Alan Schneider and Buster Keaton on *Film*. He was supposed to return to Paris on the morning of August 6, but his hosts, Barney and Christine Rosset, overslept and he missed his flight out of Idlewild Airport. A second reservation for late that afternoon was made then Beckett and the Rossets spent the rest of the day at The New York World's Fair in Flushing Meadow, Queens. At one point the Rossets lost track of the Nobel Prize winning writer and found him sitting bolt upright on a bench in the shade, fast asleep.

I was twelve when The New York World's Fair happened and it happened only a train ride away. When you're a kid, anything exciting usually happens too far away to do you any good, but this gift of the gods was almost in my backyard. I went as often as I could and might have been at the Fair on August 6, 1964. I can't prove it one way or the other. It's a fifty-fifty shot. Heads or tails depending on how you flip the radioactive dime you got at The Hall of Science by dropping your coin in a slot and watching it roll past some uranium. It came out the other end where a Geiger counter proved it was officially radioactive. They put the irradiated dime in a plastic holder and gave it to you. It was years before I started to question the wisdom of giving contaminated money to children as souvenirs.

I could have been at the Fair the same day as Beckett. I could have walked past him as he was sleeping on that bench. Gleeful corporate showmanship all around and the author of *Ohio Impromptu* put to sleep by the whole silly show. People trying to finish their Belgian waffles in the moist summer heat, teenagers selling stiff felt pennants stamped with the Fair's symbol, the Unisphere on a field of blue and orange, and the credo of the event: "Peace Through Understanding," and Sam in his overcoat, dead to the world. A narrow, angular man, sleeping upright on a bench, like a tableau at the beginning of a Beckett play. Or a tableau at the end of a Beckett play. Or, let's face it, like an entire Beckett play.

Upstairs Woody and Jeepers are looking for Boots when they encounter a federal agent, Jim Meadows, played by Richard Webb (1915–1993) who was the Ovaltine sponsored *Captain Midnight* of the 1950s. Agent Meadows is on the trail of the spies, having tracked them to the Beauregard mansion. Woody and Jeepers explain their situation.

"What proof do you have that you're an entertainer?" Agent Meadows asks Woody.

On the spot, there's nothing else Woody can do except pick up his guitar and sing another song to convince the lawman.

An hour and ten minutes have elapsed by the time the spies are smashed and our reunited trio is on the road again, back in the Pontiac in front of the same process footage that began the film, singing a full reprise of their song about the impending Nashville show.

And we're reaching for our hats because this feels like the end, but no.

The final twenty minutes of the movie are filled with the aforementioned Jamboree. One by one performers step onto a small stage backed by a generic combo and lip-sync to what we can only assume were popular songs in that brief moment of time. The performances are intercut with stock footage of an enthusiastic crowd in a much larger venue. I believe this is footage from David O. Selznick's 1938 production of *A Star is Born*. Regardless of its source, the footage indicates audiences like to dress up for their jamborees in Nashville.

Merle Haggard appears in the flesh as do two female singers, Molly Bee and Marcella Wright, both wearing minor variations of the same outfit; a one piece, blue spangled cowgirl costume topped by rhinestone sprinkled white cowboy hats. Even Don Bowman's Jeepers gets a chance, singing a novelty song about being drunk in a Levittown-like development, Mandalay Villas perhaps, and always stumbling into the wrong house.

The stock footage audience is equally appreciative of one and all.

Joi takes the stage next to closing to sing *Don't Need a Part Time Lover*, a bouncy, upbeat tune about how she wants all your attention or none at all.

She shimmers in a white and silver catsuit cinched with a silver belt. Dressed like a fifties space-chick she seems so happy to be in this dreadful movie. As Joi lip-syncs to the playback you watch her pretty face, those cheeks, the green eyes, platinum hair. Then you glimpse her throat and you realize this is a woman about to turn forty. There are the beginning of those two cords on either side of the windpipe, those tendons that show up one morning to announce the onset of middle age. But before you can completely process this indicator of mortality something truly remarkable happens.

Joi makes a mistake in lip-syncing to the playback. The prerecorded lyric is "Can't take a part time lover," but Joi has mentally skipped ahead to the next verse which goes "Can't use a part time lover."

She freezes for a fraction of a second then plows on. Looking at the DVD in slow motion you can see her start to form the wrong word. You can't turn "use" into "take," so she clicks on to the next word, catches up and finishes the song.

Beyond the heartbreakingly human glimpse this gives of Joi muddling through and not stopping the take is the fact that this mistake is in the movie. There was a decision on the day not to retake the setup and later to use the mistake instead of cutting around it. So, this stumble was immortalized. One flicker of humanity surrounded by all that creative inertia.

I had to turn on the lights in the bedroom before starting work on *Hillbillys in a Haunted House* and by the time I was finished it was full dark outside the windows. The rain drummed the roof and gutters and formed a small lake around the drain on the deck.

While the last of my tortellini warmed in the microwave I took a broom onto the deck and cleared the leaves and dirt blocking the drain. The broom made a very satisfying wet scraping sound, almost the sound of raking leaves.

While on the deck I heard my neighbor's car start and watched her back out and drive away, rain defining the beams of the headlights. I stood there and watched until her taillights went around the corner. I was soaked to the skin and would have to put on dry clothes before I could eat.

We arrive at Joi Lansing's final feature film, *Big Foot*. This low-budget tale of the search for a primitive man-beast in the California mountains carries a 1971 copyright. Some chronologies indicate Joi appeared in the film after a brief recuperation following her cancer diagnosis and surgery in 1970, but anecdotal evidence and my own suspicions suggest the film was actually made in 1969. Regardless of her recuperative powers she simply doesn't look like someone who's been hospitalized for cancer surgery in the previous six months.

1969 or 1970, before surgery or after, it was her last movie and no improvement on *Hillbillys in a Haunted House*. Making a qualitative distinction between the two films requires a fine calibration in the measurement of awfulness. *Hillbillys in a Haunted House* is the more static movie, trapped in its haunted house sets for the bulk of its running time while *Big Foot* covers more geography as it chases up and down a mountainside. But it's important to remember what *Big Foot* director Robert F. Slatzer forgot: Motion is not the same thing as action.

Shot in vibrant if unevenly timed color, *Big Foot* begins with a cluttered wide shot of several private airplanes parked near a taxi way. Acres of runway fall away in the background where mountains define the horizon.

Joi Lansing drives into the middle ground in a red convertible. We stay in this all purpose master as she gets out of the car, takes a parachute from the back seat and starts what will soon become obvious is a visual motif of the film: People walking away from the camera.

She's wearing a blue jumpsuit and seems to have put on a pound or two since her last picture. Nothing unattractive. There's simply more substance to her walk as she approaches a battered white and yellow single engine plane that looks like a survivor from the thirties.

Joi climbs aboard, sits at the controls and pulls the radio headphones over her ears. Shot inside the cabin of a real airplane there was no way to get anything wider than a very tight close-up of Joi's face as she contacts Burbank tower for clearance and starts the engine. The tight framing shows a face slightly fuller than we've seen before. She's wearing make-up, but not too much; false eyelashes, impeccably shaped brows, some blush. We're so close and the sun is so strong we can see the texture of her skin like the surface of an egg under her make-up. Shots like this can be very cruel to a forty-two-year-old actress and an experienced cinematographer might have tried to compensate with filters. That's the kind of care she would have gotten from Harry Stradling or William Daniels, but Joi was photographed here by Wilson S. Hong and is on her own in these close-ups.

The plane taxis and takes off into the sky above the eastern San Fernando Valley. Shots of Joi at the controls were made on the ground, carefully framed to avoid showing any ground or buildings through the windows around her.

Once in the air the plane is replaced by stock footage of a much smaller, newer aircraft with a different wing configuration and painted a different color. Joi looks down at the mountainous countryside below and we cut back to Earth where a battered station wagon makes bumpy progress along a deeply shaded dirt road while generically twangy country music plays. At the wheel of the car is Jasper B. Hawks, played by Joi's *Hillbillys in a Haunted House* co-star John Carradine, dressed in a dusty suit and a faithful old hat. On the passenger side is Elmer Briggs, a man with a beard worthy of a New Bedford whaler. Briggs is played by John Mitchum (1919–2001), brother of Robert Mitchum and author of the patriotic verse read by John Wayne on his album *America, Why I Love Her.*

Jasper and Briggs drive along as we cut from the exterior of the car to the interior of the car to an interior point of view of the road ahead, back to an exterior drive by, then into the car again. This goes on for almost two minutes; the men riding along, listening to the music supposedly coming from the car radio.

Eventually the car conks out. Carradine rests his severely arthritic hand on the door ledge. It looks like the gnarled root of an ancient tree. He unties the rope holding the door shut and steps out onto the roadside. He opens the back of the wagon crammed with the junk the itinerant peddlers hope to sell, takes out a bucket and tells Briggs to get water for the radiator. There's a stream right down the hill, he tells his partner, although how he knows this is not explained. Briggs starts down the hill with much folksy complaining.

Jasper stays behind and lights a cigarette. A moment and the air is filled with the insect buzzing of several motorbikes. Eight bikes, each with the horsepower of a leaf blower, rush by Jasper. On board are a clean-cut bunch of "bikers" in bright clothes and no visible leather.

Briggs reaches the base of the hill and looks around. With one cut he goes from an exterior location to a small soundstage dressed to look like California forest. There are unfamiliar animal noises and portentous pounding on a piano as Briggs discovers a series of tremendous bipedal footprints leading to the bank of the stream. Briggs fills his bucket then hears the guttural growl of some unseen animal. He quickly retreats to the spot where the cut put him in the studio and is returned to the real exterior through the mercy of another edit.

Reaching Jasper and the car Briggs warns that, "There's something out here, Jasper. I seen big huge footprints down by the stream like I never seen before."

Jasper looks at his partner and tells Briggs if he sticks with him, "You'll see a lot of things you've never seen before."

The camera lingers on Carradine's face just long enough to be awkward then we cut back to Joi at the controls of her plane. The engine sputters. Unseen grips rock the plane. Joi sends out a mayday radio call. As the craft loses altitude, momentarily turning into a third airplane, she pulls on her parachute and leaps into space. The plane crashes off screen as Joi's parachute floats to the ground somewhere in the wilderness below.

We discover Joi next to an outcropping of rocks near her chute. She starts to remove her blue jumpsuit, her blonde hair flowing around her shoulders, unruffled by the descent. Under the jumpsuit Joi wears a sleeveless tunic of a dress, open from her throat to her belt, the hem six inches above the knee. She wears gray suede boots which will be gone in subsequent scenes.

As she shrugs out of her outfit we realize she is being observed. Cut to a shot of the unsuspecting Joi seen through a pair of hair covered legs. This is accompanied by a strident sting of organ music. The hairy legs move. A threatening humanoid shape closes in on Joi. She starts to scream, the back of her hand coming to her face. The image freezes. Ten minutes into the film, the main title begins. Joi is billed second.

On the other side of the credits we're outside Bennett's General Store on a dirt road in the shadow of the mountains. The clean-cut bikers have parked their muscular Yamahas and gone in for supplies. They are a wild bunch indeed. One fellow in chinos and a blue polo shirt tries to walk off with a Styrofoam cooler under his windbreaker. Challenged, the young tough hauls off and pays for the cooler.

The bikers drive off as Jasper and Briggs arrive and enter the store. The unconvincing look and feel of the movie's exterior sets is matched by the cheap flats and meager dressing used for its interiors. Standing behind the counter is Mr. Bennett played by silent movie cowboy Ken Maynard. Once as popular as Tom Mix, Maynard, born in 1895, was a star of the 1920s who was making a reasonable transition to sound films when a series of battles with Carl Laemmle, Jr. at Universal in 1934 lead to a precipitous decline. His final years were spent in an increasingly miserable alcoholic stupor, sometimes locking himself alone in his small trailer for weeks at a time. Serious malnutrition was a contributing factor to his death in 1973.

Jasper introduces himself and Briggs to Mr. Bennett and before launching into a sales pitch asks about a beer.

Bennett tells him, "That wild motorcycle crowd just took the last can."

Demonstrating the movie's obliging tendency to cut to whatever was just mentioned in a scene, we jump from the general store to the bikers making their way along the trail with the full-throated roar of a fleet of lawn mowers.

Two bikes stop at a fork in the road. On one Chris, played by Judy Jordan fresh from a stint on the Miami Beach based *Jackie Gleason Show*, has her arms around boyfriend Rick, played by Robert Mitchum's son and John Mitchum's nephew Christopher Mitchum (b. 1943). Next to them are Wheels, the nominal leader of the group, played by one of Bing Crosby's sons Lindsay (1938–1989), and his girlfriend Peggy played by Joy Wilkerson whose lineage appears to be untouched by celebrity. Rick and Chris break off from the group and head up a side trail.

Shots of Rick and Chris riding up the trail are intercut with what look like handheld point of view shots taken by someone walking up the trail. After a minute of this we are left with little doubt that Rick and Chris did indeed go somewhere.

We find the couple in the soundstage forest reclining on a blanket. Rick is dressed as before in a yellow jacket, Chris has stripped down to her yellow bikini. There is kissing accompanied by the plaintive strumming of a guitar on the soundtrack, then Rick goes off to check on his bike. Chris lays back on the blanket and looks up. A sky photographed far from Hollywood is cut in as her perspective. She looks at the sky, we look at the sky. We look at her looking at the sky. Thoughts of Michelangelo Antonioni come to mind, but the possibility director Slatzer is making a deliberate reference to *L'Eclisse* seems unlikely.

Eventually it occurs to Chris to do something. She gets off the blanket and starts wandering through the limited confines of the small set finding a curiously carved stone the appearance of which is heralded by the same organ sting we heard over the shot of Joi through the legs of her attacker. Chris calls to Rick. Behind her we can make out the circling shape of a hair covered humanoid.

Rick finds Chris and his dialogue tells us what the film's visuals have withheld.

"This looks like some sort of Indian burial ground," he says. "They must have been giants. This one looks fresh."

Rick starts clearing the loose dirt piled on a body length mound at the base of a crude rock monument. Just under the surface Rick uncovers another organ sting and the face of a dead ape-man represented by the sort of gorilla mask Ernie Kovacs used to create The Nairobi Trio.

A similar mask watches the defilers. The furious big foot creature charges, attacking the couple. Rick is knocked unconscious and Chris is carried off.

In the midst of this action we cut to the other bikers around a camp fire, drinking, eating and making out. The dancing and groping come to an end with the crushing of the last beer can. Wheels announces it's time to go. His girlfriend notes Rick and Chris never caught up with them.

"What if something happened to them?"

Based on no information whatsoever, Wheels assures her that nothing could have happened to the couple and they're sure to catch up with them on the road home. They all start down the murky day-for-night trail.

After a stock shot of a coyote howling we return to Rick as he wakes up among the burial mounds. His girl and simian attacker are nowhere to be seen. Rick gets on his bike and after first visiting the now abandoned campsite, rushes down the mountainside alone.

Meanwhile, back at the general store, Jasper and Briggs wait for Bennett to finish with his customers before restarting their sales pitch. Just as we start to wonder why we're watching this scene Rick arrives and calmly asks if there's a phone he can use. Rick calls the sheriff's office and tells Sheriff Cyrus he better get up there.

"Something terrible's happened," Rick tells the Sheriff in a voice untainted by urgency.

We cut to the sheriff's office, another arbitrary collection of flats, where the sheriff hears Rick's side of the phone call and we don't. Perhaps it's Rick's bland reading, but the sheriff is unconvinced by the young man's story.

When the sheriff asks to speak to Mr. Bennett, Rick petulantly drops the earpiece of the wall-mounted phone. Mr. Bennett steps into the shot and picks up the phone to repeat much of what we've just heard. The only apparent reason for this part of the scene is to put Ken Maynard in a self-referencing composition with a poster for one of his old movies on the wall next to the phone.

Rick makes another call, this time contacting Wheels who's made remarkable time and has already arrived home. While Rick tells Wheels he better get right back up here, Jasper and Briggs consider the entrepreneurial opportunities presented by the situation.

"If we can catch one of those creatures we can live high on the hog for the rest of our lives."

They offer to return to the mountain with Rick and search for Chris and the creature who abducted her. Cut to bouncy country music and more shots of the station wagon making its way along the old dirt road. As the sequence stretches on we begin to suspect the movie is taking place some distance away and the characters have to travel hours to reach it.

Finally stopping, Jasper, Briggs and young Rick march into the forest. We start with the actors near the car at an exterior location, cut with them into the forest set then cut to photo-doubles in the same wardrobe and photographed at a considerable distance moving through the foothills.

The three reach the site of the burial mounds where they are observed by one of the hirsute creatures. They set off up the mountain; the classically trained Carradine, the grossly overacting John Mitchum, and the not acting, barely paying attention Christopher Mitchum.

Cutting away we find ourselves at the edge of a fog shrouded compound. We move into the mist and figures take shape, indistinct but definitely female. We discover Joi in her short dress tied to a stake at the edge of a soundstage clearing. She stands there, demurely, hands tied behind her back, bare feet turned in a model's stance. She looks like a sacrificial cocktail waitress at Ceasar's Palace.

This is the first time we've seen her since her pre-title crash almost twenty-five minutes earlier. Chris, still in her bikini, is tied to an adjacent stake. Three creatures of various sizes and genders watch them from across the clearing. Chris asks Joi about their abductors.

"They're more human than you think," Joi tells her. She believes they represent a dying subspecies who have captured human women in the hope of breeding with them and surviving in a new form. These Big Foot creatures are the missing link, she tells Chris. And there's something high up the mountain even they are afraid of.

Jasper, Briggs and Rick continue their vague progress. They stop and discuss whether to press on or wait till daylight. Inaction being easier to stage than action, they decide to stay where they are.

It takes less time to leave the area than it does to get there because a cut to what we assume is the next day shows Wheels and the others on their bikes still trying to meet up with Rick. Perhaps the mountain moved during the night.

The bikers drive on and on and we cut back to Joi and Chris and the creatures. A small, younger animal, the result of human/Sasquatch crossbreeding, is left to guard the girls while the adults go off to forage. Inside the small ape costume is four-foot, three-inch Jerry Maren (b. 1920) who as a teenager appeared as a member of The Lollipop Guild in *The Wizard of Oz* (M.G.M., 1939). He's the Munchkin who hands Dorothy the lollipop as a token of greeting.

Jasper, Rick and Briggs start searching again. Briggs asks Rick about his biker friends. Ricks says they'll be along. As direct evidence of this we immediately cut to more shots of the bikers coming along.

The photo-doubles for Jasper, Rick and Briggs press on. They climb, their backs to us to conceal their faces, starting in the middle ground or closer then moving off, diminishing, leaving us behind, getting smaller and smaller in the distance until they've all but disappeared. Then we cut to another shot of their backs filling the frame and they start away from us again, retreating with the steady rhythm of an outgoing tide. With every new departure you worry this time the movie will abandon us out here in the woods like Snow White.

Finally we rejoin Mitchum, Carradine and Mitchum on the woodsy set as they discover a giant footprint and its accompanying organ sting. The rescuers are observed by creatures lurking in the rocks above them. The trio pushes on. Close-up after close-up of them pushing apart branches and looking around until they see it! Big Foot stalking through the location footage. Jasper and Briggs react with rural aphorisms of amazement. Rick stares off into space.

They decide to follow the creature in the hope it will lead them to the girl. We cut back and forth from the camera doubles in the real forest to the actors stomping around the same few square yards of rented shrubbery on stage.

They stop once again to discuss what they'll do when they catch the creature. Rick looks at a pine cone. Then off again, unaware they've been observed by stone ax carrying proto-humans. Farther up the endless trail the three are set upon by the hairy creatures. As the fight begins we immediately abandon the action and cut back to Bennett's store where Sheriff Cyrus and Deputy Hank arrive in their patrol car.

The sheriff enters the store and recapitulates the contents of previous scenes for the enlightenment of Nellie Bennett who works at the store but wasn't around last night. Out of some misguided charity, the filmmakers decided it was important to stop the movie in order to give a minor character information we already have about the boy heading up into the hills with Jasper and Briggs.

Once Nellie is brought up to date, she asks if there might be something to the boy's story. The sheriff dismisses the notion. If there was something going on up on that mountain the ranger station would inform him.

The sheriff then rhapsodizes about how much he's looking forward to the opening of deer season. Hard Rock and Slim, two card players in the store, endorse the sheriff's enthusiasm and sense of anticipation. The sheriff and his deputy leave and, for reasons known only to the director, we remain behind in the store for further discussion of the approaching deer season.

A hard and completely unmotivated cut to the partially buried gorilla mask with its signature organ sting takes us to the burial mounds and the rest of the bikers who have finally made their way back to the movie. Leaving the mounds the bikers climb on their machines and we are treated to more general shots of them generally riding.

They ride toward us. They ride away from us. They simply ride.

They stop and ask how far they still have to go. Wheels says he doesn't know, but figures they're in for "a long haul."

Realizing they've stopped near a cabin the bikers dismount on a real exterior and approach the structure on a stage where they meet a Native American woman as well as Hard Rock and Slim. For the first time we notice Hard Rock doesn't have a left arm. He tells how he lost it in an encounter with Big Foot.

Hard Rock and Slim offer to go along and help the bikers find their friends. They grab guns and dynamite and start off.

The fog has cleared at the Big Foot encampment. Joi and Chris are still tied to their stakes, now joined by Jasper and Briggs tied to another stake and the taciturn Rick tied to a pole of his own off to one side. Several dark shapes huddle in the background.

Briggs asks, "What do you figure those creatures are going to do with us?"

"They don't seem to have much use for men," Joi tells him. "They'll probably kill all of you."

The hairy beasts growl at each other, indicate Joi and point to a snow capped mountain in an unconnected piece of film. The creatures go to Joi and untie her. She struggles, but it is to no avail. Two creatures hustle her out of the camp. Joi is fully committed to this weary nonsense. They have paid her to be a damsel in distress and by God she's going to give these people their money's worth. She is dragged off kicking and screaming. Cut to a long shot of Joi and the two hairy beasts, the first of several in which Joi is replaced by a photo-double with a mismatched blonde wig.

Since something is actually happening we cut away and find ourselves in the ranger's station where character actor and Spike Jones vocalist Doodles Weaver sits behind a desk with a bored ranger on either side of him, one reading a newspaper the other trying to look like he's whittling.

Born Winstead Sheffield Weaver in 1911, Doodles Weaver attended Stanford where he was remembered for pranks and practical jokes. The brother of NBC executive Sylvester "Pat" Weaver and the uncle of actress Sigourney Weaver he may be familiar to you as the man who helps Tippi Hedren climb into the motor boat in order to deliver the lovebirds to Veronica Cartwright, Rod Taylor's young sister, in Alfred Hitchcock's *The Birds* (Universal, 1963). Gregarious and available to his fans, Doodles Weaver died by his own hand in 1983.

There's a large window behind Doodles in the ranger station through which we see a rectangle of stage forest. Weaver is on the phone to Sheriff Cyrus, reassuring him that there's nothing he needs to be concerned about and certainly no action he needs to take about the reported missing person. Like the sheriff's office, the rangers get their share of reports of mythical beasts running all over the mountain killing men and abducting women, but there's just nothing to get all worked up about.

"Oh, we do have a report of a small private plane missing," Ranger Doodles tells the sheriff. "But we haven't found it yet."

This is probably because the search has been restricted to the interior of the office.

While Weaver talks to the sheriff one of the creatures appears at the window and looks into the office. None of the men turns around to see it. I believe the intention here was humorous.

The phone call ends and we cut to the other side of the conversation, to the sheriff's office where nothing continues to happen. Maybe tomorrow we should go up the mountain and take a look.

As with *Hillbillys in a Haunted House* this almost Warholian inaction starts to become hypnotic. But before we can completely sink into a warm narcotic state we cut back to Joi still screaming as the pair of creatures brings her to a clearing. To the unexplained sound of jungle drums Joi is tied by the wrists between two small trees in a posture meant to echo Ann Darrow awaiting her monstrous groom beyond the gates of Skull Island.

Something big and powerful moves beyond the trees. The two creatures back away as what is meant to be the king of all Sasquatch enters the clearing and approaches Joi. The giant, a full head taller than Joi, reaches toward her and strokes her blonde hair as she continues to scream and struggle, thrashing back and forth in her abbreviated costume, modesty forgotten.

Finally, frightened and exhausted, Joi faints.

We cut to the bikers and the men from the store walking through the woods. Walking and walking and walking.

The fog has rolled back at the encampment where Jasper tells Briggs they've still got it made. All they have to do is break their ropes and grab the immature beast left to guard them. In an endless two-shot they reminisce about their carnival days.

Back to Joi, conscious and screaming again. The creature is gone, but a large bear is approaching her.

The giant Big Foot stands silhouetted against the sky in a shot that's already been used twice at this point. Here it's meant to indicate his awareness of Joi's plight.

Returning to the clearing Big Foot wrestles with the bear as Joi looks on. There's much frenetic cutting of the poorly exposed day-for-night exterior footage and the stage set. In the exteriors they appear to be using a live bear. During this battle of the Gargantuas, Joi is able to loosen her restraints and run off into the forest. Big Foot kills the bear, beats his chest and bellows in Kong-like supremacy. Then, noticing his sacrificial bride has escaped, he lets out after her.

We see Joi running like a zaftig fawn through the woods. The same shot of her escape is used twice in the space of a minute. Her flight is also shown in day-for-night exterior footage of the photo-double in the mismatched wig, leaping over fallen trees and dashing through the undergrowth while guitars saw away at something that sounds like an extended riff from *Layla*.

Responding to an unspoken need to locate the bikers we cut to them on various trails in shots we recognize from earlier in the picture. The movie has started to come undone, cannibalizing itself for spare parts.

At the encampment, Rick hears the whiny complaint of the approaching engines. Several Sasquatch return to camp with their stone axes just as the bikers charge into the foreground. Freed from the stake, Jasper grabs the young

Big Foot while the other creatures run from the mob. Hard Rock opens fire as the cast staggers around the small foggy set.

After a discussion about what best to use to tie up the young beast, Jasper's handkerchief or Brigg's tie, the animal escapes rendering further debate unnecessary.

Many dark figure move through the forest. Then the humans gather at the stakes.

Rick and Chris are reunited. Rick looks as happy as a man who found a parking space close to his dentist's office. The group starts down the mountain.

For the third time we see the same shot of Joi running through the landscape. After much recycling of this shot and close-ups from earlier in the picture, Joi is captured by Big Foot. The humans hear Joi's screams and rush toward her in single file through the miniscule set.

Big Foot has slung Joi's photo-double over his shoulder and is carrying her off, ever away from the camera, shrinking into the landscape, eventually exiting the shot before we cut to our band of rescuers making moderate progress up the side of a plaster and papier-mâché hillside.

I know why this set feels so familiar to me. With its fake trees and rocks, blue backdrop and flat lighting, you realize the movie is being played on a tremendous model train layout and somewhere over that hill lurks a goliath child with a Lionel transformer.

The concepts of screen direction and geography, never high on the movie's agenda, disappear completely as we cut from Joi to her double to the same shot of Big Foot we've seen four times, to shots of the humans giving chase (or to be accurate, marching along as if on line at the Department of Motor Vehicles), stock shots of mountains, stock shots of owls and other wild life, and any trims and lifts that might have been in easy reach in the editing room the day the sequence was assembled.

You feel like you're drowning in the movie and, desperate to latch on to some constant in the chaos, you try to track Joi's blonde hair. You're reminded of finding and losing that same head as the convertible zigzagged through the opening of *Touch of Evil.*

The camera looked for her in the Tijuana night, chased down alleys, leapt over buildings trying to find her laughing in the car with the bomb in the trunk. All the time film was rolling she did what she did so well: She stayed alive in the shot. She knew how to listen, how to find her light, and not block the star.

She worked for Orson Welles. Twice.

How do you not think of that as you're being lugged around a forty-by-forty woodland set by a man in a gorilla suit?

"I worked with Orson and he asked me back."

She must have felt so tired. Tired of the long days on a bad movie, and tired at a deeper level. Did she feel that particular exhaustion, the deep in the bone weariness that comes before the profound loss of health? That unparalleled weakness that frightens you as much as it drains you.

Just before the start of my last semester of college in Albany, I went with a group of friends to an unfinished house belonging the family of one of us. We all crowded into Andy's car late one Saturday night in January and drove down to Woodstock where his parents were building a house in the woods. Andy thought it might be fun to spend a night in the "cabin" roughing it. We would sleep in the house, have breakfast, then come back the following morning. There was no other motive for the trip. It was about going and returning and that was enough.

It was an all-male excursion. I shared the back seat of Andy's Gremlin with two others, Andy was at the wheel, his dorm roommate on the passenger side smoking a pipe filled with sweet tobacco that smelled like burning cherries. None of us brought a bag; we would sleep in our clothes and return unwashed the next day. Wine, beer, fried chicken and breakfast provisions were purchased from stores on Washington Avenue before we took the car onto the Thruway.

North of Woodstock Andy got off the toll road and drove the Gremlin on tracks that grew more narrow as they cut through the countryside. The Thruway and county roads were clear of snow, but the smaller lanes hadn't seen a plow in a month. The farther we went, the less disturbed the snow and there was the adventuresome awareness that our car was not intended for this purpose.

We slid off the shoulder once and piled out to push the car back onto the portion of churned and rutted snow we thought was the road. It was crisp and silent except for the puttering car engine. No lights except the headlights sweeping the choppy snow ahead, cutting moonlike shadows, and the red taillights tinting the exhaust, illuminating our breath and faces as we rocked the car. Bundled and bearded we must have looked like trolls around a forge. There was the sense of more snow poised in the air.

The car fishtailed and threw dirty snow and exhaust in our faces as it struggled back into the central ruts. We were cold and it was getting late, but we had triumphed. Laughing and wet we climbed back into the car and pressed on to the unfinished house of Andy's parents.

It was after midnight when we arrived at the dark house sitting at the end of a quarter mile of wooded drive. The boxy shell was complete, but the inside, Andy warned, was raw and unfinished. We climbed out of the car with the remains of the chicken and groceries and stamped our shoes and sneakers on the porch.

The inside of the house felt colder than the night outside. Andy used a flashlight to pick his way into the building. There was electricity for the heater that kept the water pipes from freezing and for the outlets in some of the unfinished walls, but no lights to plug into the sockets and no fixtures.

I put a bag of groceries on a length of plywood set between sawhorses in the dining room while the others helped Andy start a fire in the fireplace.

The dining room was bayed out into the yard, three sided and mostly windows. Beyond the glass was darkness. I could see the reflection of Andy's flashlight in the windows, but not my own.

The walls were sheetrock, dimpled with plaster where they were nailed to the studs. When I looked down I could see we were standing on the sub-flooring, gray, knotty and scarred by the traffic of building. There was a table saw at one end of the room opposite the fireplace, and dirty white tubs of paint and adhesive in another corner. That and some battered, harp-backed kitchen chairs were all I could make out.

The cold made the scent of sawdust sharper than I thought possible, turning it into a potent spice.

Andy and the others huddled by the fireplace putting kindling and newspapers under a brace of logs on the grate. Once the fire caught, orange light and unstable shadows grew around the room. I could see more furniture, a sofa and chairs drawn into a ragged semicircle in front of the fireplace. We sat down, still in our coats, to eat chicken from the bucket, and drink beer from bottles and wine from paper cups.

I was in a faded wing-chair. Heat billowed from the fire warming my face, but the air around me remained frigid. Like the planet Mercury, my face boiled while the back of my head remained frozen and dark.

We were tired and wet and cold and we talked little, each of us realizing this was the limit of our adventure. The fire popped and cracked and the last crumbs of conversation fell away as we individually decided it was time to try for sleep.

I leaned my head against the cold embroidery of the chair. I was bleary from the trip, the wind and the cold, but I couldn't summon anything like real sleep. When I closed my eyes the fire played on my eyelids, making muddy red and orange shadows. When I moved to block the light I realized that would block the heat as well.

After a long time, with snores on both sides of me, exhaustion overwhelmed discomfort.

When I opened my eyes again the fire was collapsing and I had a sense of light tentatively collecting in the air around me, the way it had in Mark and David's bedroom Friday.

I stayed in the chair, motionless except for my breathing and the opening and closing of my gummy eyes. It was like climbing out of heavy anesthesia.

That's when I realized there was nothing abstract about the idea of life "slipping away." In that cold room, struggling to wake, I understood how easily existence could escape the unwary. I knew it was possible to surrender, to mentally release the idea of living and it would go. Oblivion could be obtained by simply opening your hand.

As tired as I was, as much as I wanted to sleep, I believed there was a good chance that if I went back to sleep in that chair at that moment I would never wake up again.

I sat up, my joints aching from the cold and the pushing of the car, my clothes stiff. Centering my feet and putting my hands on the arms of the chair I pushed myself up to stand in the half-circle of my sleeping friends. They were bundled in the chairs and on the sofa, collapsed in their winter coats like monks who'd fallen asleep in mid-prayer. There was more light now, but still no color.

I edged between the chairs and crossed the empty living room to reach the dining room arch and the big windows that faced east across a spread of unmolested snow varnished with ice. At the edge of the property there was a stand of trees. I wish I could name them, but I can't. They were small, round-trunked things expanding into branches that, against the gray sky, looked like a map of arteries and veins. Birch? Were they Birch trees?

I stayed by the window, watching light creep into the backyard. The world beyond looked tentative and unfinished. It seemed a pale and diluted place, incapable of surviving the day ahead.

I remember this so clearly: The planet trying to assemble itself outside the window, the sawdust spice, the cold pulled into my lungs with every breath and nesting in my bones, the sticky tiredness on my eyes. My mind drops me back in that place with increasing regularity and growing urgency. As if this scene contained some vital clue, the key to all things, locked away and hidden. It seems more detailed, more important with each visitation, but its meaning, its true meaning is still beyond my grasp. Writing about it now I feel its power, but its secrets are no more knowable than they were that morning.

I watched the dawn progress, taking on more and more reality until it was hard to believe how fragile and unsure it felt when I first looked into the yard. The morning was firmly anchored by the time my friends came back to stiff-limbed life by the dying fire. They would never know how close to not occurring the day had been.

Big Foot carries Joi into an obvious redress of the original encampment set. The humans catch up and Hard Rock takes a shot at the creature hitting him just below the knee. The animal puts Joi down during a round of reaction shots of actors who don't seem to know the camera's on them. Hard Rock fires again. Others open fire. Joi's screaming fills a soundtrack punctuated by gun fire.

Graphic bullet hits are played in close-up on the creature's body, intercut with tight shots of Joi intended to reveal something of Ann Darrow's horror at the death of Kong. The shots of Joi are from different scenes throughout the picture, but at least her face is registering something which is more than can be said for the rest of the cast. Except John Carradine who, from *The Grapes of Wrath* to *Bikini Drive-in* never took money for acting and then refused to do the job.

The wounded creature stumbles into a convenient cave. For a moment it looks like Joi might run in after him, but the other humans encircle the opening and the biker who at the beginning of the movie tried to steal a Styrofoam cooler lights the fuse on a bundle of dynamite and throws it into the cave. The characters scatter for cover as the dynamite explodes.

There's a round of impressionistic cuts to shaky shots of the forest, the mountains, some selected cast members and finally the surviving creatures beginning a march up the mountain and away from human mischief. Except for Jerry Maren, it's impossible to tell one creature from another, but in one of those monkey suits is an actress named A'lesha Lee.

Sometimes billed as Alesha Lee, Aleshia Lee or Aleshia Brevard, she was born Alfred Brevard Crenshaw, a biological male, in 1937. After surviving the taunts and terrors of growing up effeminate in rural Tennessee, "Buddy" Crenshaw made his way to San Francisco and appeared at Finochio's, the North

Beach female impersonators club, where he performed Marilyn Monroe's *My Heart Belongs to Daddy* number from *Let's Make Love* (20th Century-Fox, 1960).

Certain that the sex assigned him at birth was not his intended gender, Brevard set out to bring body in harmony with mind. He began taking female hormones in order to develop breasts and further feminize his body. Demonstrating moral certainty and remarkable courage, Brevard performed self-castration on a kitchen table covered with bed sheets soaked in Lysol.

In 1962, Brevard underwent sexual reassignment surgery in Los Angeles. This included a procedure called vaginoplasty in which the penis is removed, then the scrotal and penile tissue is inverted to form a vaginal canal. The urethra is redirected while scrotal tissue is used to sculpt labial folds and sexually sensitive skin from the penis takes the place of a clitoris.

A'lesha can be seen in wardrobe more flattering than an ape costume in *The Love God?* produced by Universal shortly before the filming of *Big Foot*. She appears as Sherri, one of the "Pussycats" hired to escort Don Knotts's character Abner Peacock and help convince the world that the virginal publisher of a bird watching magazine is actually the next Hugh Heffner. A tall, striking redhead, Brevard has eight costume changes in the movie, but no dialogue. It's the sort of part Joi Lansing used to get.

Mark and David invited me to one of their birthday parties at a bar on Ventura Boulevard not far from where I lived. The place they chose was as famous for female impersonators in Los Angeles as Finochio's was in San Francisco.

The windowless building was divided into a showroom and bar, with a second bar and dance floor in the back. During the show different "illusionists" were introduced by an M.C. made up to look like Joan Rivers. Dressed and painted to resemble Marilyn Monroe, Cher, Dolly Parton, Madonna, and other female celebrities, the young men lip-synced to recordings of the genuine articles.

At one point a white-gloved arm reached through a red curtain and a strikingly beautiful person in a dress of coruscating bugle beads stepped forward and started to lip-sync to the same playback of *Let Me Entertain You* Natalie Wood mouthed in *Gypsy* (Warner Bros., 1962). The performer copied every move of the movie's striptease and my mind shuttled back to another bar. Why was this man pretending to be an actress pretending to be a stripper so much more satisfying than watching those real women back in Pennsylvania across from The Twin-Hi-Way Drive-in? I was watching artifice on top of artifice on top of artifice, but it seemed more real than reality.

After the show I said goodnight to Mark and David who told me I could reach the parking lot without walking around the block if I went through the rear bar and out to the alley.

The back bar was almost empty when I left the showroom. There was an older gentlemen in a cranberry Chanel suit sitting at the bar and a bartender in a crisp white shirt and black bow-tie. Nat King Cole was singing *Answer Me* on the juke box as I came around a brick fireplace and saw the small dance floor beyond the bar.

There was only one couple on the floor. A beautiful, tall woman, who I realized was a beautiful, tall man, with a bubble of blonde hair, wearing a black velvet gown trimmed with ostrich feathers, rhinestones at her neck, ears and wrists, and balanced on high heels that made her tower over her partner, an impeccably groomed man in his sixties dressed in suit and tie.

At first all I could focus on was the scale of this creature. The proportions were all right, satisfyingly so, but she was so big. Big, I realized, the way women looked big in movies of a certain vintage. Women with perfect hair and make-up and costumed to accent their corseted figures.

As I got used to her size I became aware of her partner. Holding this man-made woman his face was the face of someone who had achieved bliss. How long he must have sought his dream, finally finding it here. And now, at last, the dream was in his arms. Perhaps the A'lesha Lees of the world are the flesh and blood incarnations of those bigger than life women who towered over us on the screen, the custodians of a lost female animus.

I went through a fire door and down a half-dozen steps to reach the narrow alley behind the bar. It had rained during the show and the pavement was slick from the storm. The yellow lights of the parking lot drained color from the air leaving everything a dark sepia.

I started across to the parking lot and my car, but something made me turn and look down the alley. Past the rear of the bar, next to the back entrance of the adjacent business, there was another transvestite. Tall, full-figured, red hair cascading over the collar of her shiny black rain coat open to reveal her black cocktail dress. She wore a double-strand of pearls at her throat like Elizabeth Taylor in *Butterfield 8* (M.G.M., 1960).

She was pacing, smoking a cigarette. But it was more complicated than that. There was a ritual to her movements; the way the long-fingernailed hand lifted the cigarette to the lipstick defined mouth then took it away, how she blew the smoke upward, into the yellow street light.

It was as if I'd walked into a movie. I don't mean I'd stumbled onto a set, but that I'd entered the image itself. The night, the alley, the wet-down, the monochromatic feel of it, the perfect streetwalker in the perfect high-heels, smoking the perfect cigarette perfectly. I felt enfolded by the dream that flowed like perfume from this beautiful simulacrum of a woman. I knew if I turned around I wouldn't see Whitsett Avenue. I would see a rectangular gap through which could be glimpsed hundreds of plush seats filled with people watching to see what I was going to do next. Waiting in the dark the way Gloria had waited with me in that dark room years ago.

The perfect woman saw me then, took the cigarette from her lips, rested one elbow in the palm of the other hand and looked at me across the neon smeared alley.

"Something's going to happen or it isn't."

After the explosion the human characters march onto the stage, look at the rock choked entrance to Big Foot's tomb then, without comment, turn and march off again, except for Joi, Jasper, Hard Rock and Slim. Joi lingers by the cave as a dejected Jasper sits on a nearby log bemoaning his last chance for impresario greatness.

"Well, Slim, we finally got him," gloats the one-armed Hard Rock.

Then this wobbly nothing of a movie grabs for the brass ring by giving John Carradine a crude paraphrase of the powerful curtain line that ends *King Kong* (RKO, 1933).

"It wasn't you, mister," Carradine tells the hunters. "'Twas beauty did him in."

We'll never know if this invocation was done out of love, hubris or as a lame joke. Whatever the intention, the real message is a reminder that good movies and bad movies are often about the exact same things.

Hard Rock and Slim, unchastened by Jasper's words, wander out of the shot as Joi, her long blonde hair flawless in spite of her stumbling flight through the forest, comes to Carradine's shoulder and kneels beside him.

"You think he's really dead?" she asks him.

Jasper turns to her. Perhaps his dream can be salvaged.

"Now, young lady, don't you look so sad," he comforts her. "I offer the opportunity of the lifetime."

They stand. He takes her arm as the camera pulls back and booms up.

"People all over the world will want to hear all about what you endured while you were a captive of these big foot critters. I can see it now. Beauty and the beast!"

They start to exit under the rising camera.

Joi steps off on the wrong foot and almost stumbles into Carradine as they start to exit, but she keeps her eye on her co-star and regains her footing. It's the sort of minor mistake that should automatically trigger another take, but not here. The brief corrective dance to make the exit work is part of the film.

Joi Lansing's last action in a motion picture is an attempt to salvage the shot.

They step out of frame, passing under the camera which pans up to the foggy upper portion of the set. Rocks, a twisted, leafless tree, a hill, a backdrop sky. Another Beckett tingle: It looks like somebody's doing a production of *Waiting For Godot* in the next holler. Over yonder, Basil Rathbone sits under the tree wondering why only one out of four gospels speaks of a thief being saved.

Big Foot was not released until a year after Joi Lansing's death. The film dribbled into drive-ins and minor markets in 1973 then disappeared. It managed to achieve the ranking of "Second Worst Big Foot Movie" in the Psychotronic Encyclopedia of Film, failing even in failure.

All that remained for Joi Lansing after the completion of *Big Foot* was disease and dinner theater, leading to that final month in the hospital in Santa Monica.

I have an undated picture of her sitting in a restaurant with three men while a waiter presents a bottle of wine. It's a promotional shot, probably for the restaurant, taken with one big eruption of a flash. I imagine the original hangs behind a cash register somewhere in North Hollywood. I'm guessing it's from the Seventies.

She seems diminished in this picture. The muscles and tendons of her neck are visible. Gravity tugs at the line of her jaw. She wears a white dress with spaghetti straps, the right strap, the one toward the camera, has slipped down her thin arm. She's smiling across the table at the bottle in the waiter's hands. The two men on either side of her look glum and uncomfortable. The third, across from Joi, is the only one in the picture looking at the camera. He smiles, his legs crossed, one pants leg riding up to expose an inch or two of hairy calf.

The hot blast of the flashbulb lights not only the people at the table, but the service area behind them with its stacks of saucers, a pile of cups and a glass coffee carafe on a hot plate. Directly behind Joi is a brick fireplace, painted white. There's a model of a civil war cannon on the mantel, the only item up there. Above the fireplace is the mounted head of a bull. The windows in the back wall are covered by white shutters. The shutters are closed.

The side of Joi's face shines in the flash, erasing her eyebrows and making her eyes appear smaller, her face thinner, her blonde hair washed out. If you look at the picture long enough, you begin to see, or start to believe you see, some tension in her smile. There is effort in her expression. Something I've seen in no other photograph.

Does she know she's sick in this picture?

I look at the men on either side of her, each looking away, each uncomfortable, each unknown to me. One could be her husband Stanley Todd. I have no photographs or description of Todd so I have no way of knowing. Just as I can't know where or exactly when this picture was taken. All I have are observations and the echoes of memories that are mine, not hers.

I can imagine her in that hospital room. I can fill it with light the color of an opened grapefruit as the sun goes down. I can bring the breeze through the yellowing Venetian blinds in the evening, entering with the sounds of the Pacific Ocean. I can mix her morphine with the distant rattle of the Pacific Park roller coaster south of her on Ocean Avenue.

I can put Stanley Todd in a wicker chair with tropical print pillows in a corner of his wife's room, staying close, not caring what happened between her and Frank Sinatra. Willing to forgive anything if life could just go back to the way it was before. But he's there because I want him there, not because I know.

I imagine there was a point she knew she was going to die in that room. But I can't know if that knowledge came with clarity or terror. I know she died in the evening of August 7, 1972. Afterwards she was taken up the coast to the cemetery in Santa Paula. I'll repeat the last few miles of that trip tomorrow after I pack, clean the dishes, and put the sheets back over the furniture.

After the cemetery it's back to Los Angeles, and the intentionally illconcealed smiles of Mark and David.

MONDAY

In the dream, I'm in Mark and David's tub when I hear the sound of glass breaking. The tub is full and the jets are running full blast, but the water moves like something thicker than water, like some transparent pudding. It weighs more than water and it holds me down. I'm afraid to move because I don't want to find out I can't.

I'm facing the shower which is where the sound of breaking glass comes from. There's a crack in the glass wall running up from the base like inverted lightning. As I watch, the crack grows and spreads, making a sound like the tightening of a violin string.

Both showers are running, filling the glass box with white mist. There's someone in the shower. The person's movements under the spray are languid and feminine.

I think, "It must be Joi Lansing in the shower."

I strain to see details through the steam. Hair up under a blue towel, wide hips, skin pink from the heat of the water. Her back is to me.

The longer I look, the more I doubt it's Joi in there. She died more than thirty years ago. I'll be seeing her grave in a few hours. Maybe it's her ghost. Do Mormons believe in ghosts?

The crack climbs and forks, reaching for the top of the shower frame. In the dream I close my eyes because I know what's going to happen. When the crack reaches the top of the frame the shower will shatter, the tempered glass blossoming into a million marbles like the restaurant window, spraying out over the bathroom, over me trapped by the thick water in the tub.

But at least that will release all the steam and, reacting to the shattering of the glass, the person in the shower will turn around and I'll be able to see who it is.

That's when I woke up.

I stripped the bed and put the sheets in the washer, then I packed my bags and straightened up the bathroom. When I came downstairs to put the bedclothes in the dryer I saw a white corner under the front door. Someone had tried to slide something under the door the way Reef Holloway got his "save the world" orders while making out with Joi on the sofa.

I opened the door and saw it was a square envelope, the sort that comes with greeting cards. I opened the envelope and took out fifteen crisp twenty-dollar bills. There was a slip of paper around the money, something from one of those "to-do" pads that stick to refrigerator doors. Written on the paper, in some haste, was the word "Sorry" in blue ball-point ink. Nothing else. Just three hundred dollars flat and fresh from an ATM and a one word apology for something.

I thought it must be for Mark and David. A neighbor saw life in the house and stopped by to repay a debt. I put the money and note in the envelope then slipped the envelope into my back pocket behind my wallet.

After I finished the last of the Cheerios and milk and orange juice, I put the cartons and empty box in a Vons bag with my weekend's trash to be carried to the recycling bin. I took the sheets out of the dryer and remade the bed. Then I put the other sheets on the living room furniture I'd uncovered and walked around the house one more time, like a murderer inspecting the scene of his crime for incriminating evidence. I found none. There was nothing to indicated I'd ever been there. I locked the house and the gate then took my bags to the car.

Coming around the hood of my car I saw the driver's side mirror hanging against the door. It had been snapped off at the base, the plastic cracked and the mirror itself in shards on the cement. The wires controlling the mirror's motor were the only sinews attaching the limp thing to the car. There was blue paint on the cracked plastic and a line of the same color in a thin crease along the length of the door. The Volvo was gone.

Now I understand the money. Late last night or early this morning, my neighbor broke the mirror with her car when she pulled in or pulled out. She went to the cash machine at MILK-LIQUOR-LOTTO, got three hundred dollars, put it in an envelope, pushed it under my door and left.

Her house looked as shut as Mark and David's and I knew she wouldn't be returning. I suppose the anonymous nature of the apology was to keep me from figuring out who broke the mirror, but I know who did it.

I threw the bag of trash over the fence of the house next door then loaded my bags into the car.

I drove away. Past MILK-LIQUOR-LOTTO, past the Mandalay Generating Facility and PictSweet Mushrooms to get on the 101 heading north. The transition to the 126 came up faster than I expected and I had to swoop across two lanes in time to make the exit, horns blaring at my back.

I took the 126 east toward Santa Paula, past track houses and lemon groves. The mountains south of the groves are old and dark green. The storm was gone and the sky was an intense winter blue.

The 126 becomes Korean War Veterans Highway before reaching the town of Santa Paula, self-described "Citrus Capital of the World." The town and its population of thirty thousand, seventy-percent of which identifies themselves as Latino, recently suffered the indignity of being removed from the daily weather map printed in The Los Angeles Times. The paper decided that if you knew the temperature and rainfall in nearby Hesperia you pretty much knew what it was like in Santa Paula.

The access road to the Santa Paula Cemetery is off a residential street where seventies ranch houses crowd older California craftsman homes with deep porches that give them a heavy browed scowl. On the access road you can see the small cemetery off to your left, to the right is a stand of old eucalyptus trees shedding great slabs of gray bark.

I wore my long black overcoat instead of my hooded jacket in order to appear more respectful when I went to the office in a clapboard cottage set by the side of the road as it forks out into the cemetery grounds. Joi Lansing is buried in plot 444, Section N and the woman in the office had to pull a roll of frosted celluloid from a shelf in an open safe to show me how to find the grave. She unrolled the brittle map on a table in a room crowded with sample urns and monuments. In a small rectangle at the extreme west corner of the map the name "Joi Lansing Todd" is neatly printed, sideways to fit the space.

The woman helping me asked no questions about why I was looking for this particular grave. I thought she might challenge me and ask by what right I was here. I don't know why I expected she would, but she didn't. She simply told me how to find it.

I drove from the office to the section, got out of my car and walked up the gentle hill that climbs to the western boundary of the cemetery. There are few headstones in the Santa Paula Cemetery, almost every grave has a flat marker set level with the ground.

Beyond the cemetery there's a lemon grove with a white metal windmill, the sort that looks like an airplane propeller. The southern edge of Section N is a low cinderblock wall guarding a culvert that drains the run-off from the grove.

It was crisp and breezy and the tails of my coat flapped behind me. From the town there came the sound of shunting trains.

Her stone is in the shade of an avocado tree planted on the other side of the culvert, but with branches that reach over the ditch and dapple the sun falling on her grave. The stone, which has an aspect ratio of approximately 1.85:1, has only her stage name and no dates. It is meant to look like a star on the Hollywood Boulevard Walk of Fame: Her name above a star with a movie camera at the center. It is marble set in concrete.

And there were flowers. Completely unexpected flowers. A bouquet wrapped in clear plastic secured with a yellow ribbon tied in a bow and resting on the ground just below the marker. Twelve daisies, twelve yellow mums, three white carnations, sprigs of lavender statice, sprigs of baby's breath and some greens. No card.

Someone had left flowers.

I stared at the marker and the bouquet trying to comprehend the meaning of this. When I finally looked up, past Joi's marker, I saw the stones for the two graves next to hers for the first time. The far one is the marker for Carlton Wasmansdorff, the man whose last name Joi had when she arrived in California, with the dates 1904–1975. And next to Joi, the marker for Virginia Shupe. There are no dates for Virginia, but there is an inscription: "Loving Mother of Joi and Larry."

Larry?

Who's Larry?

She had a brother?

My head snapped up and I turned to look back at the road and my car as if expecting to see this Larry walking toward me through the graves. But there was no one. A wobbly plastic pinwheel clattered over a grave a few rows away, spinning in sympathy with the propeller behind me in the lemon grove. It was barely eleven in the morning and I had the cemetery to myself.

Had Larry left the flowers? Or someone else? They didn't look like they'd been left out in last night's storm so they must have been placed this morning.

I looked at Joi's stone, at the marble star. I don't know how long I stood there.

A gust of wind pushed a cloud in front of the sun. I heard a thump and looked down. An avocado had fallen from the tree. It rolled against the side of my shoe and stopped, as dark and green as the mountains to the south.

I had failed to find my mark. It was supposed to hit me on the head.

Oh, Joi, forgive me for not understanding what you've always been trying to teach me.

I looked at the flowers on Joi Lansing's grave and my heart cracked with the certainty of what I had long suspected. The simple, crystaline fact that explains my entire life:

I am in someone else's movie.

The revelation of my status at the edge of the frame lifted a great and unrealized burden from my chest and I took my first deep breath in a very long time. How much more pleasant it is to dance with Joi at the margins of the drama while Nat King Cole sings on the juke box and plot is left to more important players.

Was this the piece of cosmic wisdom that freed you after a month of hard dying in that hospital room, my beloved Joi? The knowledge that it was better to be at the edge of someone else's movie than to be at the center of your own.

To be unnoticed, but immortal.

Suddenly dizzy, I sat on the cinderblock wall and looked at her grave. I can't stay too long. There are plans to be made. I need to go to Salt Lake City, locate the Shupe family and the Wasmansdorfs, and hopefully track down Larry. But I'll sit here on this wall a little while longer.

Whoever left these flowers might come back.

0-595-33590-X